A CUP OF GLOOM

ALFIE & ANNABELLE

DEDICATION

For Ashland and Lily

A Tale of Two Letters

Which did I want first: the good news or the bad?

Actually, there wasn't really any news at all. I already knew what was inside both letters when I spotted them in the recesses of my mailbox, hiding from the January drizzle. By some cosmic joke, the State of Oregon had sent me both notices on the same day. And, of all days, on my forty-ninth birthday. Score one for the bureaucracy gods. They were on their game today.

Only one way to solve this conundrum. "Reef, here boy! Momma needs you."

The black pug, two years old last spring, launched from the cottage steps and tore down the muddy driveway. Skidding to a stop at my galoshes, he looked up expectantly at his red-faced momma. About the height of a Coke machine, she hadn't had her hair colored since Nixon, but didn't much mind the random gray shoots. She was a tad stouter than when she'd plucked him from the pound in '81, but was generous with the kibbles and polite enough to save her crying for after dark.

A letter in each hand, I bent down within sniffing distance. "OK, which one first?" Unlike me, a champion second-guesser, Reef didn't hesitate. He lunged and licked my right wrist.

No surprise there. Powered by irrepressibly positive pug DNA, of course he picked the Board of Elections notice. The dog biscuit in my right pocket might've tipped the scales, but, hey, a sign's a sign.

"Let's go inside and have a look." With a sigh, I shut the creaky mailbox and trudged up the gravel drive.

Built with his own hands by my father in the '30s, the cottage has been my home since I was a child. Anchored at the cliff's edge of The Cove, it towered over the rocky beach below. On mornings like this, I was grateful for Dad's craftsmanship. The pitched roof, the sturdy back deck, even the nautical-shaped windows were all original. Just like him. My father, a man among men. Over a pint or three, Uncle Frank used to insist the town should've been named after him regardless, tragedy or no tragedy. But Frank's gone. Everyone's gone.

The rain's din subsided as I closed the door. I pulled a chair for Reef at the kitchen table so we could review his choice. Since his reading skills were still a work in progress, I read the letter aloud.

From: The Oregon State Board of Elections

To: Mrs. Genevieve Boyd

1 Peninsula Drive,

Boyd's Cove, Oregon

November 13, 1983

Congratulations!

The State of Oregon has officially certified your mayoral election for a second three-year term starting March 1, 1984.

Although this is an unpaid position, the Governor greatly appreciates your commitment to public service and is confident you will continue to provide outstanding leadership to the community of Boyd's Cove.

Good luck!

Alfred Hill

Oregon Election Commissioner

Well, thank you for the kind words, Mr. Hill.

I pushed the note aside and added it to my growing "mail purgatory" pile, a stack too trivial to keep, but sure to bite me in the ass if I threw it away. I'd wager a similar heartfelt note from Mr. Hill after my first election was buried in there too.

After being swept into office three years ago by a decisive 151-to-141 vote, I holed up in 1 Peninsula Drive for days, cursing Sheriff Leslie for nominating me against my will. Her political instincts were frighteningly good. "They'll vote for your last name," she had told me. "Doesn't matter if they couldn't pick you out of a lineup. Now, if Anna Nixon were running, we might have a problem."

There was no problem. She thought my victory was hilarious. And now, three years later, the joke's still on me. Another term, courtesy of the good folks. Oh, and yes, there were no other candidates this year. But, that didn't stop forty citizens from writing in their own choices. Glad to see Sasquatch still has a half dozen constituents.

Oh well. At least the pay reflected the town's expectations.

The second letter, thicker than the first, beckoned. Draped atop a sofa cushion, Reef had lost interest (he hated paperwork) and was gnawing on a chunk of rawhide. I was on my own for this one.

Buzzy rumors would undoubtedly sprout, especially since I was sure the postman wasn't delivering much mail from the Oregon Judicial Department of Family Law within The Cove. The crisp documents disguised the train wreck of my ex-husband's rotten deal, buried in a thicket of clinical governmentese.

Final Judgment of Divorce Settlement Agreement

I WAS UNNECESSARILY informed that:

> The marriage contract entered into between the two parties as of July 1, 1968 is hereby set aside and fully dissolved.

THE "DISSOLUTION" BOX on the form was dutifully checked, putting a belt and suspenders on *Case # OR47850, Boyd v. White.*

In hindsight, Jerry never had a chance. We'd met twenty years ago in nursing school in Oregon's Rogue Valley, a sunny, cowboy-kind-of-place. He'd hated nursing from the start and ditched it to join me and The Cove fishing fleet. To everyone's surprise, he took well to trawling. After a season as a greenhorn, he was promoted to engineer, and then first mate. Although an outsider, Jerry played the mysterious stranger role, Clint Eastwood-style, earning the town's respect, and in a few short years, acceptance.

Our final year together was gut-wrenching. He could do nothing right. I drew hard lines on the big stuff (*no kids—not ever!*) and on the day-to-day nonsense (*Sundays are for gardening, not football!*). Against all odds, at this very kitchen table, he made one last-ditch plea to save us.

Jen, I'm here for you. I'll always be here. Your mother, your father, they left, but I won't. Just trust me. Trust us. We can make this work. We just need to try.

A heroic attempt, but he'd given me the opening I was looking for.

My father? You have the balls to bring up my father? Well, he didn't exactly LEAVE, did he, Jerry? He was KILLED! Killed in the prime of his life. He set the bar high, and you didn't even come close to it.

In case he wasn't getting the message, I helpfully drew a bar in the air above my head with my finger. My close was extra vicious, the words cold and final: *I'm not done trying, but I'm done trying with you.*

Ouch.

In the end, it was polite. We agreed to just separate so he could stay on my health insurance. On a warm July day near the end of blackberry season, he loaded up the Subaru and headed north on 199, back to Medford.

And that was that. For years, nothing. Until a couple weeks ago, when a honey-voiced attorney called to tell me to expect papers.

Did I have any regrets? Honestly, I'm not sure. My marriage reminds me of high school algebra class. A few impressions linger: the teacher's toupee, a fire drill that saved me from a pop quiz. But the specific memories vanished long ago, like a hazy, early-morning dream: you remember the cast but not the plot.

But that's it for regrets. I still have to explain the "Mrs." title when I file my taxes, but hey, *c'est la vie.*

Am I a happy person? Happy enough, I guess. It's amazing how uncomplicated things can be if you just don't think about them. Day to day, I've mastered the art of keeping my mind blank, and leave the ruminating to others.

But since we're friends now, I'll let you in on a secret. There's one recurring mind-dragon I've never been able to slay—and doubt I ever will. Before my marriage, before my prom, before even my First Communion, the Expectations serpent perched on my shoulder and has been whispering in my ear ever since.

How can you be so weak? You're the daughter of a hero. Courage is in your blood. Buck up!

If that didn't knock me flat, the next volley always did the trick:

What are you thinking? You can't do that. You're a child of mental illness. Go back to bed.

Ah, the blessings and curses of expectations. On one hand, they drive us. They're the fuel we need to succeed. On the other, they're also the great white shark that smells our blood and doesn't care how big our boat is.

Being raised in the shadow of greatness isn't the lottery ticket it might seem. It usually doesn't end well. Ol' Winston Churchill endured his son Randolph, an alcoholic who wrote a few books but mostly just bothered people. Henry Ford begot Edsel, and, well, we know how that turned out. Preston and Margaret Boyd graced the world with me, and I'm sure they'd empathize with Winston's and Henry's predicament. Despite holding a surname worthy of naming a town after, I've lived down to every expectation ever had of me. For every teaspoon of pride, a tablespoon of shame.

So, if you're thinking of trying this at home, I must say that my Thoreau-inspired strategy of hiding from the world has largely worked. But be forewarned: to play this game, you've got to be OK with anonymity. OK with being the rolling credits at the end of the movie nobody sticks around for, content to pet your dog and drift along in the jet stream of other people's plans for you.

During normal Boyd's Cove times, it's easy for me to avoid the whispering reminders that I need to do more with my life. I see the same five people, shop at the same two stores, drink the same brand of vodka (Smirnoff). But over the next few weeks, I'll be hostage not only to the demands of my one true friend but to the entire town, and everyone in America who owns a TV. Like that old Motown song warns, there's nowhere to run to, baby, nowhere to hide. Deliver, or else. Don't f-it up.

Sigh.

My hermit status is officially in mortal danger. But at least there was one thing to be grateful for this morning.

No birthday cards cluttering up my mailbox.

Boyd's
Cove

Corner Booth

Anchoring Boyd Cove's "business district," the heat-free Fog Cutter Café fooled no one by pretending it was a bistro. During a re-model a few years back, the owner Eddy, (not his real name, but his Old World tongue-twister had too many vowels for us Boyd Covians), tacked on "Café" to the moniker. He even set out a tiny French table on the front sidewalk so bait-crusted fishermen could imagine they were denizens of the Left Bank, sipping aperitifs and nibbling on wedges of Roquefort.

By any measure, the experiment failed. The table was inside by September, and everyone except the Yellow Pages still just called it The Cutter.

Regardless, I appreciated the time capsule from my high school days, right down to the red-and-white checkerboard tablecloths. The joint was laid out shotgun style: booths on the left, a counter with three stools to the right. A prehistoric jukebox, unplugged for a decade, guarded the bathroom hallway. The back corner booth was where you proposed, were proposed to, or grabbed one last patty melt before getting the hell out of town. A faded mural of the Klamath Mountains lured in malnourished backpackers from the Oregon Coast Trail. That was The Cutter, right down to the "Sorry, We're Open" sign in the front window.

I parked my Ford Bronco in front of a busted parking meter and headed inside. But first, a namaste nod to Blanche, perched in her usual spot on the neon *Fog Cutter Cafe* sign above the doorway. As always, the chunky gull—her breast stained with marionberry from yesterday's unsold pie—pretended not to notice me. Ever since Blanche had lost her right talon in a fishing line incident, she'd sought sanctuary at The Cutter. Kind of a sorry town mascot, but what did you expect? Heads turned as the door's jingle bells announced my arrival.

SHERIFF LESLIE WATSON had already staked out the corner booth. In the irony of all ironies, despite every adult's confident prediction, she'd dodged juvenile hall and joined the other team. My mother nailed it years ago: the kids who wound up cops were the same ones carving their initials into detention desks. But the day they tossed their caps at boot camp graduation, the slate got wiped clean. Duty, honor, and all that.

As a teen, Leslie got us both chased out of The Cutter for teasing the owner. *Hey, Eddy, how come you only got three stools at this counter? Where are our dates supposed to sit, in the can?* Exploding with laughter, we ditched our fountain Cokes at the counter and spilled out onto the sidewalk. Arm-in-arm, we skipped down Main Street, smug about what bad asses we were.

Those were dark days for me, as my mother's drinking descended from snorkeling to scuba diving. Leslie—and, I guess, The Cutter—gave me just enough air to break the surface.

Eddy was long gone, done in by decades of Winstons and mouthy teenagers. His son Marco manned the griddle these days. Marco's real name was a snarl of consonants that required Americanization. Once, while he was taking my order, I asked why a purebred Frenchman with Burgundy-red blood had settled on an Italian alias. I never got an answer, but did pick up a few new French expletives.

"You're late. Urgent town business, I assume?"

We both knew that wasn't true. At least I'd made it. Last week I'd blown off breakfast, buried under the covers with a hangover that deserved its own headline. Leslie didn't ask for excuses. It was just Jenny being Jenny. Of course she'd already ordered for me. I waved to Marco and slid into the booth, ready for the rest of my beating.

Suddenly, a new waitress appeared, carrying two plates smothered in Denver omelets and half-cooked hash browns. For us regulars, a new girl on the floor was a big deal. Not a lot of employee turnover at The Cutter. No Cadillac pension plan waiting on the other side, no management training program—just bone-on-bone arthritis and a web of kitchen-burn scars.

I grimaced in sympathy. The oily-faced youngster should've been busy failing geometry, but a junior prom pregnancy had taken care of that. High school had been Disneyland compared to this circus. So much to learn! She'd need crash courses on Lyle Whitmer's extra Tabasco needs and Shelley Brady's diabetic menu. Those quarter-century-old toilets weren't going to clean themselves, and good ol' Blanche didn't just sit on the Fog Cutter Cafe sign all day. Careful, sweetie, don't spill the vinegar and soap while you climb the stepladder.

"They're the same order, hun. Just give us either one." It always baffled me when Leslie was more courteous to strangers than to me. Actually, it made sense. She'd had VIP seats for all my shitty decisions over the years. Hard to put down the judgment stick after you've helped your divorcée friend pack for "just a short stay" at the nuthouse.

Leslie stared as I mixed my omelet with my hash browns. "Please tell me you haven't forgotten. I realize the agendas for our weekly sheriff/mayor meetings haven't exactly been packed, but come on, Jenny!"

I decided not to remind her again that she wasn't an actual sheriff. But the boys at County let it ride, treating it more like a nickname than a title. If she weren't so good at her job, no doubt it'd be a problem. Personally, I thought "Chief of Police" was a fine title on its own. But she leaned into the gunslinger image, small-town western lawman and all that. So, "Sheriff" Leslie Watson it was.

And no, I hadn't forgotten.

Leslie wasn't taking any chances. "In a week, all the mucky-mucks from Portland will be here. And you'd better get your hair done for the CBS interview."

I chewed my food as what little patience she had fluttered away. "I'm sure they'll do a 'man-on-the-street' segment. Have you identified any of these local yokels who can put two sentences together? God help us if Edie Brower finds her way to a camera."

She wasn't done. "Oh yeah, and dig up some pictures of your father and mother. CBS can't keep your tongue-tied mug on screen the whole time."

Smiling in spite of myself, I snapped off a mock salute. "Aye, aye Captain. Understood. I'm actually headed to an interview now. Permission to shove off?"

"I'll shove you off if this stuff doesn't get tight," she growled. "Who's the interview with?"

"*The Courier.*"

"Ha!" she exclaimed. "That'll be a great tune-up for the network next week. Let me guess—"

"No need. Yeah, we're meeting at The Barnacle."

She shook her head in disgust. "Well, Keegan will be easy to find. Last stool at the bar, closest to the pisser. That is, if he even remembers."

Leslie pushed her clean plate to the center of the table and tossed her napkin on top. Other than Reef, she was the fastest eater I'd ever seen. With a little-too-hard pinch of my bicep, off she went.

The check and I remained behind.

Mom and Dad

Across the street from The Cutter, The Barnacle Saloon is Boyd's Cove's longest-running Broadway play. Think *Cats* or *Evita*. It's the same show every night. If you saw it in '82, you saw it in '83. Individual actors age out and move on, but the script never changes. Your Barnacle tap choices are (and always will be) Budweiser or Rainier. You'll read the same raunchy toilet graffiti you giggled at on your eighteenth birthday. But despite the bad reviews and tired songs, the play survives for another season, as long as the Cove keeps supplying fresh batches of thirsty dead-enders.

Old Man Keegan was strictly a Rainier man. I suspect he's also responsible for some of the saucier bathroom jingles. Editor of *The Coastal Courier*, Tom Keegan was about the same age as the paper's circulation (I'm rounding up here) — 300. His celebrity avatar? Let's go with cranky Mr. Roper from my favorite guilty-pleasure sitcom, *Three's Company*.

The paper's masthead promised two issues a week—a pledge as dependable as a Caribbean flight schedule. Foreclosed upon years ago, Keegan moved *The Courier's* operations to The Barnacle (as the lead story that day truthfully explained) "to be closer to our sources." Mission accomplished.

Every two years or so, The Barnacle's deed changed hands. New owners quickly realized that charging a quarter for yesterday's flat draft meant a trip to bankruptcy court. Or, in the case of the last two, they spent too much time sampling the suds themselves. In search of some much-needed ambiance, one of them gussied up the place by installing tempered-glass portal windows from an old fishing boat on the front door. Built to withstand waves, weather, and fed-up wives, they were among the few surviving relics of the kitchen grease fire of '69.

Stale cigarette smoke and the sour, yeasty smell of decomposing beer let me know I was in the right place. No one at the every-seat-taken-at noon bar looked up as I walked in, but I didn't blame them. Sally Jessy Raphael, queen of tabloid TV, was clucking away from the set stashed high in the corner above the Old Crow bourbon supply. How would the stepsister love triangle play out?

"Down here, Boyd!"

Don't you love it when people call you by your last name?

"I see you, Mr. Keegan."

Well, sort of. A cloud of Marlboro Red fumes seared my eyes as I made my way to the back of the bar. As an ER nurse, I'd been exposed to every part and parcel of Cove crud, so I rarely got sick. Still, the filthy faux-leather booth seat gave me pause. With an invisible sign of the cross, I slid in anyway. To my surprise, Keegan wasn't alone. What the hell? He was always alone.

The old hack reveled in my astonishment. "Let me introduce you to my apprentice, Ms. Jessie McBride."

"It's Jessica." The rail-thin brunette nodded but didn't extend her hand. She was young, maybe twenty, but IDs were optional here at The Barnacle. Hair pulled back in a no-nonsense ponytail, her black-rimmed Carrera glasses perfectly accessorized her ivory button-up blouse. "And I'm not his apprentice. I'm here on an internship from U of O."

I couldn't resist. "Are you last in your class?"

At least Keegan found that funny. Ms. McBride did not.

"No, Mayor, I *chose* this assignment. Good to get out of the city once in a while."

I let the fib slide. "So, Tom, Jessica, I'm here. What do you want to talk about?"

Keegan claimed honors on the first tee. "Well, it's only a week away. Six nights and a wake-up. Forty years, huh? Don't see what's so damn special about it. Feels as arbitrary as pulling a random foreign village out of a hat and slapping 'sister city' on it."

I smiled with my mouth, but not my eyes. The Boyd's Cove—Zihuatanejo partnership from a few years back still bugged the hell out of him. Maybe he was right. Other than a sign on the freeway ramp and a basket of Mexican candies, the town didn't have much to show for it—except for my predecessor's scandalous, all-expenses-paid trip south of the border, which got me elected.

Cub reporter McBride was done with pleasantries. She had a story to write, dammit.

"Mayor, let's start at the beginning. Can you please take a look at this?" She pushed a mimeographed sheet of paper in front of me, like a prosecutor presenting evidence to a hostile witness.

I glanced at it, but knew the November 22, 1942 Oregonian article by heart.

<table>
<tr><td>BREAKING
NEWS</td><td style="text-align:center">The Oregonian</td><td style="text-align:right">BREAKING
NEWS</td></tr>
</table>

<table>
<tr><td>VOL. 10, NO. 4</td><td style="text-align:center">SPECIAL EDITION</td><td style="text-align:right">22 NOV 1942</td></tr>
</table>

ENEMY SENDS USS STRYKER TO ITS DOOM

On Sunday evening, the USS Stryker, a salmon-class submarine commanded by Captain Preston Boyd was torpedoed and sunk by a Japanese vessel. All thirty five hands save one is feared lost.

Feared lost? No, Captain Boyd, my father, was definitely lost. As were my mother and I for many, many years.

The engagement took place approximately three miles due west of Salubrious Point.

Lucky me. From the Pacific-facing bay window of my childhood home, I had a daily view of WWII's only house call off the Oregon coast. As a child, on clear days I'd peer across the brine at the featureless patch of sea where the battle was fought. I'd imagine it was the Japanese, not the Americans, who met their doom on that cloudless night. And my father, heroic vanquisher of the enemy a stone's throw from Uncle Sam's shores, would be the first down the gangplank, searching for me in the crowd.

But at bedtime, I'd wrap myself head-to-toe in a scratchy wool blanket, cocooned like a mummy against the howling winds. As the night wore on, I could never quite convince myself that "it's only my imagination" when the sound of sailors' terrified screams pierced through the fierce, whipping gale.

The town council voted to rename the local municipality "Boyd's Cove" in honor of Captain Preston Boyd.

Random moments are what I remember most about my father. Spreading hot shaving lather on his face one morning. Slapping Aqua Velva on his damp cheeks. Putting up the storm windows in the fall, right before Halloween. Hating the sight of him in his Navy dress blues which signaled yet another deployment.

It was different with my mother. With her, there were no seasons, only sameness. After my father's death, I'd mix her daily 4 PM Canadian club and tonic, and toss in a lime if we had one. At the crack of the ice cube tray, she'd come downstairs, exhausted from doing nothing. After carefully setting the tumbler on the TV tray, I'd sprinkle a few pretzels on the side.

But no soaps or game shows for her. Instead, the channel was set to the bay window station, a commercial-free, endless oceanic tundra with the sound turned all the way down. I was off-duty after that, each of us free to hibernate in our own corners of the cottage, grateful to be unseen by the other.

Deegan came to Jessica's rescue. "Is there a question you wanna ask the Mayor?"

The Boyd's Cove carpetbagger cleared her throat. Apparently, the overachiever had written out her questions in longhand and was determined to read each one verbatim. Wonderful.

"Yes, of course. Mayor Boyd, next week marks the 40th anniversary of the sinking of the USS *Stryker,* just a few thousand feet from American shores. Other than Pearl Harbor, the worst military disaster in US waters of the entire war."

Was there ever going to be a question?

"As mayor and daughter of Preston Boyd, captain of the USS *Stryker*, are you excited for the commemoration ceremonies next week?"

Keegan rolled his eyes. Really? A yes/no question? What were they teaching in journalism classes these days?

Let's see. Was I excited to relive the murder of my father and his merry men?

No, my dear, I was not. But not for the reasons you might think. I'm not worried about dredging up old memories. I'd shoved them way down years ago. And I'm not the Nancy Drew type. Never felt the need to revisit all the blank gaps in my weird, f-ed up past. Does it catch up with me sometimes? Yeah, it does. Bet yours does too. Bottom line, I've grown to like my little life, one grocery run and dog walk at a time.

But this town is a cove, not an island. Like it or not, it belongs to The World. And The World, like a manta ray that needs to keep swimming to breathe, never rests. It's a tornado, incessantly beachcombing for the next Elvis or Three Mile Island to entertain itself.

And now Boyd's Cove was in its path.

Tell you what I *am* excited about. The day this circus packs up and you grifters scurry back home. But I shushed myself. Tornadoes feed on turbulence. Moist air slams into cool and before you know it, you've got a supercell thunderstorm on your hands.

I needed to keep my act tight here. Be boring. Forgettable.

"Why yes, Jessica—may I call you Jessica? I'm very excited about all the media attention surrounding this important event. It's inspiring to know that because of reporters like you, Americans who may never have heard of the USS *Stryker* and its brave men who gave their lives for our freedom will finally learn of their sacrifice."

Thankfully, no follow-up. On to the next scripted question.

"Next weekend will be packed. A parade down Main Street, a ceremony at *Stryker* Memorial Park, a Blue Angels flyover. But the most significant event will take place five miles north of town on Sunday when you and other dignitaries break ground to start construction on the newest Coast Guard base 'Air Station Boyd' named in honor of your father. How do you feel about this base and how will it affect the lives of everyday Boyd Cove citizens?"

Another minefield I wasn't about to cross. Ms. McBride would never realize it, but she'd just brushed against the real reason the whole world was about to rent every Impala at the Medford airport, buy a map with a scale large enough to include Boyd's Cove, and get carsick on Route 199 for two hours.

After a decade of lobbying (and a particularly deadly fishing season), the Coast Guard was finally getting its new base: helicopter squadron, search-and-rescue training facility, the works. With the nearest Kmart fifty miles away, the current Boyd Cove mayor wasn't sure the area could support an additional 500 souls. Her phone calls to the governor were eventually returned (not by the governor of course), assuring her how careful the planning had been and thanking her again for her father's service on behalf of a grateful nation.

But if a new military base is built and no one hears about it... well, that's political malpractice.

Cue the Coast Guard PR machine. Apparently, the news cycle in 1983 is so moribund the Coasties managed to rope in *60 Minutes*, the highest-rated TV show for the last ten years, to get in on the fun.

I can hear the pitch at CBS. After years of recession misery, let's take the country's mind off of its troubles. America, meet Boyd's Cove! First, we'll revel in the faded glory of a long-forgotten WWII battle, *pro patria mori* and all that. Then, cut to today's heroes, the USCG, as they carve a new base out of the frontier wilderness (nothing controversial about the Coast Guard, everyone loves them). All that's left to do is fit Harry Reasoner for a new London Fog slicker and fire up the plane.

My interrogator tapped her Bic pen impatiently on her yellow legal pad. This interview would be good practice, isn't that what Sheriff Leslie said? Fine. Let's test-drive this response.

"The entire town is *thrilled* with our new Coast Guard neighbors. With all this open space, we'll barely know they're here. Recognizing the service of my father and his men by naming the base after him is one of the greatest honors of my life."

Lois Lane appraised me as I dabbed at an imaginary tear. Putting her pen down, she crossed her arms and cocked her head to the side. Was I really that bad of an actor that I couldn't even fool this greenhorn? Reasoner was going to grind me up like fresh pepper.

The next query came unscripted and landed like a haymaker in a heavyweight prize fight five seconds after the bell. Maybe there was a future in media for young Ms. McBride after all.

"Mayor Boyd, can you share a personal memory of your father?

What an idiot. How could I not have anticipated this one? With no heartwarming Mayberry-style anecdote at the ready, I was forced to tell a true one. Keegan gleefully noticed my squirming and almost put down his drink to listen.

"Sure, Jessica. We had a signature father-daughter game that we'd play once in a while. Now, you may find it a little twisted."

My nervous laughter was met with silence. Off to a great start.

"Anyway, after dinner I'd sit at the kitchen table and get lost in my favorite *Phantom* comic book. Father would sneak off to his bedroom and put on a rubber Creature from the Black Lagoon mask he'd gotten from Woolworths. Like any good submariner, he'd lurk soundlessly in the background until the spookiest part of my comic. Then, just when the Phantom was about to finally confront the villain, the Creature would strike! With a hideous screech, Gill Man, as he called himself, would pop up from behind my chair and sink his hands into my shoulders.

"Of course, I'd run out of the room screaming, and the Creature would pursue me with a Frankenstein shuffle. I'd lock my bedroom door, but I'd hear the murmurings from the other side.

"We come unseen, Jenny Boyd, we come unseen."

In nursing school, I learned arrhythmias and cardiac arrest are uncommon in eight-year-olds. I beg to differ.

Jessica started to ask her next question, but Keegan grabbed her wrist. The old fart knew the best parts of any story always come at the end. Now struggling with real tears, I felt compelled to finish.

"At his funeral a year later, as the air still echoed with the crack of M-14 rifles, I told this story to his commanding officer. He took off his cover, bent down, and told me something I never forgot. 'Genevieve, do you know where the phrase *we come unseen* comes from? No? Well, it's the Royal Navy submariners' motto. Your dad loved the Navy, and he loved the submarine fleet. He was always complaining that the British submariners had a motto, but we didn't. That's why he came up with a motto for his own sub. He loved that idea... the idea of being unseen.'"

The old man and I had that in common.

I could feel the sense of relief from the other side of the booth. After enduring my inane non-answers, *The Courier* finally had a touching public-interest angle for their story. I shook my head, like Reef does when he resets himself while searching for the perfect place to pee. Can't let that happen again.

Jessica again. "Last question. What was it like growing up in a town named after your own father? After all, you're sort of a mini-celebrity around here. And to lose your father, and then your mother? It must have been very hard..."

She let the question trail off, just like *60 Minutes* would've done. Nice try—but you've already gotten your one honest answer today from this old lady.

But, dear reader, since you've come this far I'll put my cards on the table. I may bitch about being mayor and being trapped in some unpublished Edgar Allan Poe novella. But that's just me humbling my pie. Truth be told, I enjoy my unearned status in town as the unofficial town daughter. Within these few square miles, the family legend still lives. Boyd library, Boyd elementary school, the memorial obelisk in the town square—this town remembers and honors its version of the past.

And, as a result, it remembers me. I don't cash in on the currency of my last name too often. I don't wave to the crowd from Mr. Donaldson's Model T during the 4th of July parade or say things at council meetings like "I think my father would have wanted us to do it THIS way." I'm more like Pacino hiding in plain sight on Melrose, with the pulled-down ball cap and security walking ten steps behind.

The biggest benefit of my surname might surprise you. After my mother's death, I'd sought answers to the big existential questions. But, forays into everything from Christianity to mysticism all failed to explain why a forty-five-year-old mother with a teenage daughter would choose to stride into the black surf and drown herself. In the year of our Lord 1952, ten years to the day after the death of my father, I joined the ranks of orphandom.

Eighteen years old, angry and adrift, I almost followed her myself. The months after her death were a blur of visitors, signing papers and Leslie sleeping over, afraid to leave me alone. Meanwhile, Boyd's Cove stepped into the breach. The town paid off the cottage mortgage, and enrolled me in nursing school. Every detail was handled, thoroughly and anonymously.

So, I owe Boyd's Cove a debt no honest person could pay. Best of all, upon my return from college, the town minded its business. No expectations were imposed—which I embraced: go to work, come home, rinse and repeat. It took me a while to realize, but to the town, I was a fragile, hothouse flower. After I kicked my husband to the curb, the Cove unofficially assigned itself as my Sir Lancelot, blood-sworn to slay any future outside Dragons that dared appear.

But Dragons did come. Anxiety, depression, and paranoia befriended me during my twenties. There were years of barely leaving the cottage: sleepless nights, then weeks, that even my mother's Canadian Club couldn't cure. Let's not forget to mention that summer night after midnight (I've never even told Leslie this), I found myself on the beach, staring into the crashing surf towards Forget-Me-Knot Rock, convinced I could reach it, not caring if I didn't. Sprinkle in an eating disorder that said hello every couple years, and, voilà, with apologies to Mr. Springsteen, darkness was no longer confined to the edge of town.

Where does this leave me now? You're probably not surprised to know I don't believe in therapy. It's psychobabble that only invents new terrors to add to the ones you already have. My forty-five years of expert conversations with myself have led me to the following things I think I think.

Shakespeare's genius was consequences, always consequences. Deny your child her chosen lover? Prepare to lose her forever. Full of ruthless ambition? It will ruin all you hold dear. The House of Boyd extracts its own price. It shelters, but also imprisons. I'm somebody here, nobody out there. Venture too far from its walls—say, Portland for nursing school or Medford to seek forgiveness—and the signal weakens, then disappears.

Better to stay in my ditch and be happy lying in it. The risks are just too great. Lose your identity, lose yourself, and who knows, maybe, like your mother, you'll lose yourself into the sea.

A Discovery

Pulling into my driveway, I knew what to expect. Sure enough, Reef's little black head popped up like a prairie dog in the window and disappeared as if bopped with a Whac-a-Mole mallet. Cracking the door open, I half-heartedly fended off his slobbery greeting and the buzzing puppy energy. No one else was ever—ever—this happy to see me. I hopscotched to the kitchen as the mutt wove in and out of my ankles, playing his favorite game: "Trip the Old Lady."

Reef wasn't a natural beach dog and the Cutter regulars never let me forget it.

Pugs aren't cut out for the outdoor life!

That wombat would make a perfect wolf snack.

And my personal favorite: *Why don't you get a German shepherd? Single woman, living out there all alone. You need a protector, not a lap dog.*

A 24-7 October drizzle had overstayed its welcome into early November. Bothersome, but not too bad. Wet enough for the ground crew to sand the basepaths, but not dire enough to call off the game. No way Reef was letting me off the hook. For him, our daily beach walk was a core course, not an elective. But first things first: lunch bunch time.

"Down Reef, down, it's OK." I'd cured him of his yapping fits during meal prep (*Remember, only babies bark!*), but had long since surrendered to the rest of his lunchtime shenanigans. Standing on his hind legs, he pawed at my thigh, clamoring for his bowl RIGHT NOW. I rotely scooped out the entrée—a scoop of Alpo mixed with white rice and mushy carrots—then rolled my eyes as he inhaled it, joyously licking the sides for every last smidge of gravy.

My turn. My silver coffee pot, a Sears catalog special, had survived every Goodwill purge and even outlasted my husband. It percolated more slowly than my newer one. But coffee's for savoring, not speed. I'm not even sure I need to actually drink it; after forty-nine years, the earthy smell of a fresh dark roast with its caramelized sweetness and touch of bitterness rivals any of life's pleasures, up there with a so-hot-you-can-barely-stand-it bath.

Stroking Reef's shiny black fur, I took my first sip.

Ah, strong, black Navy coffee, just the way I liked it. Fortified, I drifted into the cabin's so-called family room to take in the ocean view (yes, I know I don't have a family; I still call it that—stop judging).

I'd stalled long enough. Time to walk the dog.

Without too much grunting, I pulled on my black Totes overshoes and stepped through the back screen door. From the landing of the wooden staircase, the entire windswept beach stretched below. Tucking the little dude under my arm, I yanked up the collar of my Irish wool sweater and tiptoed down the slippery steps with that hyper-aware middle-aged caution every over-forty knows. At the bottom, I set the squirmy pug down and scanned the cove.

The tide was out this afternoon, resting in its full diastolic phase, retreating well past Forget Me Knot rock. A spectral curtain of fog had descended earlier in the morning, walling off the shoreline from the sea. After parking at the water's edge, the gloom had put up its feet and settled in, like your shoes-optional uncle in his recliner at Thanksgiving. Muted by the briny haze, the day's colors slowly drained, blending into the silvery horizon.

Why was I shivering so much? The onshore wind had died down and it's not like I didn't know what to expect. I'd carried two previous dogs down this staircase and combed this beach for decades, so a little weather was nothing.

If I started feeling sorry for myself, I knew what would happen. My father's voice would boom inside my skull: *Why, Jenny Boyd, you've no right to be cold! There's no such thing as inclement weather—only inappropriate attire!*

Well, my attire today was ship-shape. With my slicker, galoshes and two thermal layers, I was northwest Sherpa, chic, if there was such a thing. Maybe Leslie was right—my ass is getting old and this wind doesn't mess around.

Enough of this fascinating self-conversation. I turtled my hands into my sweater sleeves and looked around, half expecting snowflakes. Visibility was poor, five, maybe ten feet at most. Not ideal. Down here alone, it could get dangerous. Boyd's Cove wasn't Central Park at sunset, but it had its own brand of coastal mayhem: slippery, moss-covered boulders, collapsing seaside cliffs, and the occasional beach-camping vagrant on his way to Alaska.

Best to keep these winter walks short. Let's get this over with.

Reef, of course, had zero concerns. Heedlessly picking his way towards the water, he paused at every fishy smell and rock-crab sighting. Though already well marked on previous visits, he insisted on re-staking his territory, tail wagging wildly as he scrambled down the pebbly beach.

Just ahead, the squawking of a half dozen circling gulls grabbed our attention. Never one to miss a party, Reef let a few pug-woofs fly and bounded toward them. What fresh horror had washed up now? Buttressed by cliffs on three sides, The Cove was a magnet for ocean debris. Over the years, I'd seen all types of creatures wash ashore: sharks, bottlenose dolphins, even a baby Orca back in '78. Calling all gulls! Tired of hunting krill and mussels? Feast like kings at the rocky graveyard of Boyd's Cove!

Now I had another reason to shiver. My pug had vanished into the fog, lost among the tide-carved rockpools. Where had he gone? No barking, no trail, just a swirling gray haze and the constant hum of the ocean in the background, droning like a 24-hour freeway.

"Reef! Where are you?" I bellowed faithlessly. Unsurprisingly, silence. At times, I doubted he even knew his own name—although, admittedly, there was strong circumstantial evidence to the contrary. Selective hearing was the more likely culprit. His ears would reliably perk up at magic phrases such as "Chicken Dinner Time!" or "Let's gooooo for a walk!"?

At least the gulls heard me. They hear everything. From high above, the circling flock shrieked back in unison, vanishing and reappearing in the vaporous mist. I squinted at the gray sky. Yup, my instincts were right. They were hovering, zeroed in on something further down, where the shore met the sea.

Threading my way through the abalone-encrusted boulders and tidepools, I reached the squawking canopy of seabirds. Then I froze. Something moved in the shadows between two slabs of driftwood. Sure enough, there he was, the little rascal! Curled low and silent, he was almost invisible save for the faint glint off his slick, raven-black fur.

I wasn't the only one shivering. My fearless wingman, famous for bullying the local pit bull, was trembling like a stranded seal pup. His front legs stiffened as I scooped him up, his heart racing so quickly I could have taken his pulse through my long johns.

What the hell was going on? Why was my little tough guy so terrified?

Then I heard it.

A moan. Low, ragged and undeniably human, it rose from behind a stack of driftwood, snapping the hairs on my neck to attention.

Planning to write a job description for a position in Boyd's Cove? Better include "world-class imagination" under essential skills. Nights here are long here, the days even longer. No HBO and, sorry to say, only one pizza delivery option (spoiler: it's not that great). Around here, entertainment isn't something you outsource—it's a DIY project. Some folks call my imagination dazzling. Others... well, they call it grounds for trazodone and lithium.

So you can understand why it took me a moment to believe, a long frozen moment to sink in. Time slowed as the world narrowed to this single, impossible scene. As Carl Sagan famously said, "Extraordinary claims require extraordinary evidence." Well, my, my—this was truly extraordinary.

I set Reef down, and he tucked himself behind my legs as we both stared at the body.

Twenty years as an ER nurse helped cushion my shock. I'm no stranger to death. Truthfully, it doesn't particularly bother me. Put in twenty years at the Curry County ER, and you might feel the same. The dozen or so drowning victims I've tended to have all blurred into one. Gray, unseeing eyes. Sloughing skin. Engorged lungs. The coroner's report practically writes itself.

No medical training was required to pronounce this poor lad forget-the-CPR dead. A young man—a boy, really—lay on his back, his vacant, dead-fish eyes fixed on the sky. The incoming surf gently tugged at him, but he belonged to the beach now, his left shoulder wedged beneath a slate outcropping. Clumps of spongy, dark kelp clung to his torso and feet. Boots on. Belt buckled. No sign of crabs or sand fleas. Definitely not dead long.

True, Jenny. But dead long enough that there's no way he could've let out that moan—or was it more of a sigh? I let out a deep sigh of my own. The wind was picking up now, tilting toward a cross-shore direction. OK, it's decided. No looking back. Dead things don't moan, groan or sigh. Reef and I are officially the only sentient beings on this beach. Natural explanations only today please. Could've been a sea lion fight on Forget Me Knot or Reef practicing his ventriloquism. Or a forcibly retired nurse just hearing things. Wouldn't be the first time.

The alternative? Not worth considering. Plenty of reasons why. The cross-eyed look I'd get from Leslie tops the list. Not to mention reacquainting myself with that bottle of expired trazodone tucked in the shoebox at the back of my closet.

No. Let's leave crazy out of this.

As the gulls settled on a nearby boulder and feigned indifference, I bent down for a closer look. He couldn't have been in the water long, maybe a few hours. No evident postmortem decomposition, no facial scrapes from the stony ocean bottom. I touched his cheek and neck. Pliable, no rigor mortis. Just that waxy, pallid feel of the dead. His standard-issue US Navy denim coveralls were drenched, and clung to him like a second skin. The cold fabric smelled of salt and something faintly metallic. His breast pocket bore a black name tag etched with gray lettering.

Well, hello Seaman Hayes.

Wish we could have met under better circumstances. Bet you do too.

Were there others? The cove stretched end to end for a solid mile, and searching the entire crescent by myself was beyond me. I scanned the surrounding area—the rocks, the kelp, the tide pools—but found nothing. Relieved, I returned to Seaman Hayes. Where'd you come from son? Any ID in your pockets?

I brushed the kelp from his face and chest. Pinned to his lapel were three silver bars: Seaman First Class insignia. The edges of a shoulder emblem peeked out, partially hidden beneath more kelp. I pushed the seaweed aside and leaned in closer. Shaped like a medieval crest, the patch was emblazoned with two crossed swords with a narrow orange flame flickering between them. Along the top, the motto read: *Silentium Est Aureum.*

Silentium Est Aureum. Silence is golden.

I gasped and sprang to my feet. Backing away, I stumbled on the wet rocks, nearly falling on top of poor Seaman Hayes. It wasn't possible.

Breathe. Just breathe.

It was no use. It was the bad old days all over again. And here I thought I was done with all this—but no. Not even close. First came the palpitations, pulsing faster and faster, pounding in my chest. *Deep breaths, Jenny. Deeper. It's the only way.*

No use. My vision narrowed and blurred, warning me of what was coming next. Sure enough, the gut-wrenching nausea hit like a punk rock warm-up band, determined to make me forget about the headliner. Thrown into dry heaves, I collapsed to my knees. Retching fiercely, I donated my coffee breakfast to the beach and gulls. With a revolting spoiled milk aftertaste in the pit of my throat, I closed my eyes, desperately willing the assault to pass.

After a few minutes, the worst was over. I wiped my tears and curdled dribble on my sleeve and staggered to my feet. Reef was gone again, but this time I could see him. He'd taken advantage of my meltdown to do some unsupervised exploring. I looked down again, as if it would make a difference. Nope. Seaman Hayes still lay prostrate before me, blissfully undisturbed by my emotional stigmata.

Confirmation was needed. Yeah, I'd read it right. The insignia did indeed proclaim *Silentium Est Aureum*—the motto of the USS *Stryker*. The motto my father had come up with. The motto of a forty-year-old wreck, lying a half mile underwater, about three miles as the crow flies from Forget Me Knot Rock. Divers had been banned from poking around the vessel for decades. It's an official military cemetery, like the USS *Arizona* at Pearl Harbor. Below rest thirty-five souls, entombed in this submerged boneyard—including my pop, Captain Preston Boyd.

But I guess I'll have to redo the coroner's math on this one. Because unless my eyes were deceiving me, this morning you'd only find thirty-four.

An AWOL Sailor

What a relief.

I didn't figure it out until I'd gotten back to the cottage.

After all, logic was far more efficacious at stopping anxiety attacks than Xanax. And I owed this revelation to my answering machine. As I picked up the phone to call Sheriff Leslie, I noticed the recorder blinking red. That's weird. My machine was never full. When you average only one or two calls per week, you rarely need to flip the tape.

Except next week was no ordinary week. Saturday marked the ruby anniversary of the *Stryker*'s demise, forty years to the day she last surfaced. Suddenly, producers, photographers and Coast Guard aide-de-camps were all clamoring to talk to the mayor of Boyd's Cove. Most never got past "this voice message machine is full." I was needed for once. All these interviews, sound bites and press releases weren't going to generate themselves.

And who knows? As the '50's, '60's and '70's age out to become the romanticized "good old days" and high schoolers can no longer name our half-dozen wars since Hiroshima , this might be the last big hoohah for the USS *Stryker* boys.

So, what better way to bring it all to life than a re-enactment? Maybe not on the scale of the Gettysburg centennial, with a regiment-by-regiment recreation of Pickett's Charge. But it wouldn't take much. A few creative souls could dry-clean some WWII–period uniforms from their attics, exhume a preachy historian to nail the period details, and—bang!—suddenly it's 1942. Sketch out a downtown parade route, and, just like that, you've got some stirring footage for the *60 Minutes* crew and their geriatric audience.

Mystery solved! Seaman Hayes must have been a naval actor, conscripted for a patriotic costume party. This new-found clarity settled both my stomach and my mind. How did he end up on my beach? Well, that was indeed a mystery... but, happily, not mine to solve.

Nope, pass that baton to Sheriff Leslie. She pulled up minutes later in my gravel driveway, her civilian Jeep Cherokee's dashboard light flashing blue through the fog. She'd taken the doors off when she bought it five years ago and never put them back on. The lone Curry County ambulance, fifteen years old and overdue for an oil change, lumbered in behind her. Leslie plopped her Smokey the Bear hat on, then changed her mind and tossed it into the passenger seat.

Hands thrust in the pockets of her Pendleton corduroy jacket, she was all business.

"Just what I need. You sure he's dead?"

I just looked at her.

"Oh, excuse me, Nurse Ratchit. Forgive my silly question. I forgot you see floaters everyday out here on Forget Me Knot."

I let it slide. "He's dead alright. And not for very long."

"Alright, alright, lead the way."

The late afternoon sky had distressingly darkened since Reef and I made our discovery. Not much daylight left, maybe an hour. The two EMTs set their stretcher down on the bluff's grass and hustled after us, looking more like sixth-period study hall refugees than participants in a potential murder investigation. I took point, leading the way towards the corpse.

The sky above the body was empty, devoid of gulls, as the tide inched its way out. Calm earlier, the wind now whipped around me, heralding the arrival of yet another wintry front. Out across the Pacific, storms stacked patiently behind one another, waiting their turn like an afternoon plane lineup at O'Hare. I pulled up the hood of my raincoat and tightened it against the chill as I approached my second rendezvous with Seaman Hayes.

"About twenty yards this way, over here by the—"

I stopped myself. We'd reached our destination. Or at least I thought we had. A familiar, gut-tightening déjà-vu rose in my throat as I confronted the inconceivable.

The body was gone. Gone. No trace it had ever been there. Disappeared. Vanished. Extinct. No blood. No footprints. No animal tracks. The shallow tide pool where I'd found the Seaman Hayes impersonator just an hour ago lay pristine and undisturbed, waiting for a fresh surge of seawater. A crime scene without a victim.

Was this the spot? I must be confused.

Except I wasn't. I'd grown up in the faded mustard cottage on that bluff right there, overlooking this cove. Over the decades, the world had been carpeted over and mutated into an unrecognizable neighborhood where only the house numbers remained the same. It wasn't mine anymore. But not this beach. The same prehistoric boulders I'd scrambled over as a little girl were still here, unmoving and unmovable. My mother and I had even given names to the larger rocks. *I'll meet you at Theodore in a few minutes.*

And, sure as hell, Hayes had washed up right here, wedged smack between Claudius and Athena.

OK, whoa—let's break this down. What happened to the body? High tide was at least two hours off, so scratch that from the suspect list. A good samaritan? Not impossible, but I didn't often see my octogenarian neighbors braving a freezing November beach walk at dusk. My stairway was the only way down from the bluff. No one else could have been here. No one.

Undoubtedly (and understandably), I could predict The Law's working hypothesis: a jaded, burned-out nurse loses touch with reality. Probably off her meds. Happens all the time. Can we go now? It's taco night at the station.

Leslie crouched low over the beach where Hayes's head had lain, her mocha windbreaker's fur collar pulled up to her chin. She picked up some stones and let them slip through her fingers, listening to the soft clatter as they hit the sand. Reaching into her pocket, she tapped a Skoal tin, then shoved a Texas-sized wad of chaw beneath her lower lip.

I backed up a few steps, bracing for her first spit. Growing up, we'd done almost everything together, but even the entry-level "get-the-teens-hooked" mint green snuff was beyond me. Peppermint Juicy Fruit was the most mutinous substance I'd ever dared put in my adolescent mouth. Besides, it doubled as a Budweiser mask in case my mother got too close during bed check.

The EMTs exchanged uneasy glances, then shot wary looks at Leslie. My breathing came in gulps as I paced the inlet, searching for a sign—any sign—of my AWOL cadaver. Invisible gulls mocked me from above with their sharp cackles, as if they were in on this macabre magic trick. Blinded by the fog, I stumbled into an icy late-breaking wave and was soaked to the bone.

Call it. Breaking point reached. Bruce Banner Jenny morphed into the Hulk, right then and there.

"Impossible! Fucking impossible!" I stalked the beach, shaking my head. "He was right here! Maybe the tide took him out."

"Try again, sister." I knew what Leslie meant. The tide had barely moved since my discovery. Hysterical, I called out for him, as if he were Reef or a golden retriever.

"Seaman Hayes! I know you're here! Where—"

I turned to Leslie.

"He's somewhere on this godforsaken cove! Maybe out on Forget Me Knot Rock?"

The fog muffled my voice and the look on Leslie's face sobered me up instantly.

"Someone must have moved him!"

Leslie wasn't having it. "Interesting theory. Now, who do you suppose could have done that? In the hour or so since you left, a Squatch came down from the hills, plucked a 180 pound body off the beach, and disappeared without a trace. Not sure that flies either. What do you think, boys?"

The EMTs were smart enough to keep their mouths shut.

More tough love came my way. "Look Jenny, this is either some Stephen King ghost story or you're confused."

My silence invited her to pile on further.

"Yeah, you're right, the laws of nature have been temporarily and supernaturally suspended. Or..."

Leslie grabbed my arm gently and steered me away from the first responders. Out of earshot, she softened slightly.

"Look, I'm not sure what you saw—or didn't see— here this afternoon. But I do know a couple things."

She paused, locking eyes with me, the calm authority of a parent about to impart hard-won wisdom.

"We both know that over the years you've had three or four 'breaks' with what the shrinks like to call *the real world*." She italicized the phrase with her fingers, just in case I wasn't getting the message.

"Also, these last couple of weeks have been nuts, no? I'm no brain mechanic, but I'm guessing that with all the attention lately on your dad and the *Stryker*, maybe some of those fun old family memories you've been keeping stuffed down decided to come out and play?"

She'd gone this far; she might as well finish. "Look, this whole zip code is a weird f-ing place. If you'd asked me to play Nostradamus back when you were in the middle of all your shit, I'd have put my money on you ending up as the town sea hag—not a nurse, or, for Chrissake, mayor!"

The pep talk was over. "Here's what's going to happen next. I'll look into this, see if there's any distress calls or missing people. As for your Seaman Hayes, as far as I know there's no *Stryker* costume parties planned. In the meantime, you're going to get yourself together, march your ass back home, and keep your mouth shut. Capish?"

Leslie didn't wait for an answer from the chagrined town sea hag. She marched off the beach, the two EMTs scrambling to keep up. I slumped onto a tree-sized piece of driftwood, letting the sand shift beneath me. Maybe a half hour of daylight left.

Alone in the cove, Reef and I combed the shoreline, all the way out to the point. I clocked piles of kelp and a gigantic rotting lingcod, but no sign of my vanished guest. After an hour of futility, a northwest Gulf of Alaska wind drove me back toward the beach stairs.

"Breaks with the real world," that's what she'd called them. The language in my medical chart put a clinical spin on my brand of nutso. Apparently, *psychosis triggered by trauma* explained my *delusions*—that I was being tailed during nursing school by a cadaver I'd dissected in the first semester. Throw in *hallucinations* of my mother drifting through the cottage at night, out the back screen door, and vanishing over the edge of the cliff. Oh, and let's not forget the episode that cost me my nursing license: confronting the werewolf ICU patient.

Yeah, not exactly the most reliable witness to put on the stand.

As Reef and I approached Hayes's empty parking spot, he noticed the commotion first. A buzzing cloud of shore flies swarmed over my stomach's earlier offering. Crabs and other creepy crawlies scuttled frantically, looting the dwindling remains. A couple of sniffs later, Reef moved on, already thinking of the after-walk cheese puffs in his future.

But not me. Maybe there was no body, but my puke was the next best thing—physical, incontrovertible proof of my experience. I HAD seen a body. His name WAS Seaman Hayes. USS *Stryker* insignia HAD been pinned to his lapel.

But... why now? And why me?

I'm not sure about many things. Even my doubts have doubts. But this I knew: there was a tether between me and this Seaman Hayes, whoever he, or it was. I could feel it, deep in my chest. Some sort of cosmic mirror had cracked. Its reflection promised nothing—nothing but the truth. The truth behind the black hole voids in my life I've never understood and never outrun.

Library Learnings

I still had an hour.

Dodging rainwater-filled potholes, I tore into the unpaved parking lot of Boyd's Cove library. Despite owing its existence to a long-dead congressman, the library still ended up bearing my father's name. Like most libraries, more attention was paid to design than function. The ocean wave-inspired roofline won the architect an award, but inside was as cramped as a submarine. Painted-over cinder block walls were lined with dusty portraits of former librarians, shushing from the Great Beyond.

Fortunately, Eva Brown, librarian et al., took her job seriously. The microfiche machine actually worked and finding the card for the November 22, 1942, Oregonian front page took only minutes. I drew a steadying breath and slid the card under the lens. A twist of the knob brought that horrible day into focus.

The familiar headline splashed across the front page, bigger even than The Oregonian masthead itself.

| BREAKING NEWS | The Oregonian | BREAKING NEWS |

VOL. 10, NO. 4   SPECIAL EDITION   *22 NOV 1942*

ENEMY SENDS USS STRYKER TO ITS DOOM

This caption always struck me as tabloidish, but that's certainly what happened. I scrolled down, hunting for the part I needed.

The list of missing is as follows:

I froze. And then gasped. Straight off the teletype, in alphabetical order, 10th name down, there it was: *Hayes, Foster. Seaman First Class.*

In my life, I've known some Befores and Afters: Before my divorce, Before Reef, After my last negative scan. But this one trumped 'em all. And now, thanks to *The Oregonian*, I had a new entry: "Before seeing a ghost."

"Noticed you're digging into some family history. Brushing up for next week's festivities?"

How long had she been standing there? "No, Eva. Just browsing. Can I help you?"

Eva Brown—librarian, town busybody, and self-appointed guardian of Curry County lore—peered over her glasses. Crumpled by osteoporosis, her spine was locked in a permanent stoop, a posture tailor-made for her favorite pastime: peering over patrons' shoulders.

Ignoring my *leave me alone* vibe, she continued.

"You know, with all the upcoming events, I'm surprised I haven't seen Mr. Quinn's name on any of the guest lists. I'd have thought he'd at least be in the parade."

As mayor, I was fluent in passive-aggressive small-town code: those "tsk-tsk, why don't you do something" jabs dressed up as innocent questions. So some guy I'd never heard of wasn't in the parade? Somehow that was my fault? Omniscience was apparently part of the job description. Just last month I'd been blamed for not foreseeing the possum population boom.

I stared at the microfiche screen. I'd read it right. Hayes was still there, still missing, according to the manifest. At least until 1600 hours today.

"Genevieve? Genevieve, are you alright?"

Eva's hand on my shoulder brought me back. After a couple deep breaths, I switched off the machine, and turned to her. To buy time, I picked up our conversation midstream.

"Yes, yes, of course, I'm fine. Just a little dehydrated, that's all. Appreciate your concern. Now, who's this person you think should be in the parade?"

Like all narcissists, Eva took the bait. "Mr. Quinn. Liam Quinn. Surely you must know who HE is?"

I sat back in the chair, gaining control of my senses. Grateful for the distraction, I played along. "No, 'fraid not, never heard of him."

Now it was Eva's turn to be dismissive. "Liam Quinn? He's the sole survivor from the *Stryker*. Served under your father. Comes in here from time to time."

Eva had my attention. "Liam Quinn? He survived the battle? And he lives here, around these parts?"

She elaborated, "Well, maybe it's not surprising you don't know him. He's pretty reclusive. He lives way up in the Bald Hills—Wolf Mountain, to be exact."

She stopped herself, searching for the perfect question to squeeze the biggest nugget of gossip from me. "And I must say, I am surprised you don't know him, given your family... history. You mean to tell me that no one in this town, not even Sheriff Watson, has ever mentioned him to you?"

Yes, that is what I mean to tell you. My turn to ask a few questions.

"You said he comes to the library once in a while. So, with your friendly personality, you must know him a little. What's he like?"

Eva appreciated my fake compliment. "Well, as a matter of fact, I do. He's older, maybe mid-70's, but in good shape. Takes care of himself, all that outdoor mountain living must do him good. Pretty sure he lives by himself."

"Good to know. Nice person, easy to talk to?"

The librarian glanced around, making sure no one else was in earshot. In a conspiratorial whisper, she cautioned, "Actually, he's a pretty cantankerous old coot. Dumped over a book cart in here a few months ago when he found out he owed dues."

I thanked Eva and stood up to leave. As I was saying goodbye, I mused aloud, "You're right, I wonder why I never knew that. And, why would people not tell me? It's almost like it was being kept a secret."

For an instant, that "I've said too much" look crossed Eva's face, her eyes flickering before she looked away. But she was hardwired to speculate, and the temptation was too strong.

"You know, Genevieve, this town, like all towns, has its secrets. And I know most of them. But secrets aren't always bad. I'm guessing, but most people probably just felt like you'd dealt with enough. Shielding an eight-year-old girl from a constant, living reminder of the most tragic night of her life is... well, I guess, a form of mercy."

I let Eva close in for a goodbye hug. Two weeks ago—or even two days ago—I likely would have welcomed it. But it all comes down to the secret itself. A good secret, an *honest* secret, can withstand the full light of day. A bad secret, though, crumbles in the sunshine, like Vlad the Impaler at noon.

What kind of secret was Seaman Hayes?

Mirage

"**B**RRRING!" One of the last rotary dial phones in The Cove welcomed me as I walked in the door. I switched on the entry table lamp and looked for Reef. From his couch perch, the pug lifted his head, saw it was only me, and curled back up to resume his siesta. I set my purse down and lifted the receiver.

"Hello?"

As always with Sheriff Leslie, my greeting went unreturned. We had nothing in common except the important things. Two of the last holdouts from our high school class still in Boyd's Cove, we'd both come back home after checking out the world east of the Siskiyous to get-dark-early afternoons and sideways rain.

Right to the chase. "No reports from Eureka to Astoria of any missing ships, sailors or sea lions. All quiet on the western front."

I tilted at one last windmill. "And no *Stryker* reenactment actors?"

An exasperated sigh. "Girl, I already told you. No re-enactments on the schedule. Put that one away."

I stared at the phone. The safety net of a plausible explanation was gone. Seaman Hayes—no, his name was Foster, Foster Hayes—was not on that beach. He'd never been on that beach.

"So what now?"

"What now? Well, that's up to you now, isn't it?" I heard her spit into her dip bottle through the phone. "Options are pretty frickin' clear. 'A,' go tell everyone at The Cutter you're finding perfectly preserved 40-year-old corpses no one else can see. Or, 'B,' maybe just sleep it off, dry-clean an outfit for *60 Minutes*, and don't f-up this whole shindig in honor of your father. Not a tough one for me, but then I'm not the one seeing imaginary shit, am I?"

One last try. "If all that's true, how the hell would I have conjured up a detail like his frickin' name out of thin air? And the *Stryker* patch! Explain that one, Sherlock!"

Leslie didn't hesitate. "Here's what I think: at some point over the past forty years, you must have read that manifest list and seen those names. Now, I'm not saying you memorized them, or even *remember* seeing them, but isn't it possible that some of those names—maybe even only one—got embedded deep into your subconscious?"

"And, boom, here we are, on the eve of this huge memorial. And all the compartmentalization that Jenny Boyd, the captain's daughter, was so good at for so long—keeping the nightmares downrange, far away— well, the walls start to come down. And from the very back of that thick skull of yours, a long-forgotten name, good ol'Seaman Hayes, leaks out into that five percent of your brain you actually use."

The line was silent for a moment. "Now, I can't explain how your wires got crossed from there. But it's either my explanation, or it's Elvira story time at The Barnacle."

Defeat. The debate was over. My hard-won grip on reality, reacquired at such a cost, was gone. A mirage, a house of sticks, toppled by the anniversary of an event that occurred before most of the town was even alive. The weak prefer illusion. Count me among them.

My calls with Leslie always ended with her hanging up without saying goodbye, so I quickly asked my other question.

"One more thing. What do you know about Liam Quinn?"

Silence, then a long sigh. "He's a crazy old bastard who lives up in the Wolf Mountain treeline. During the wildfires a few years ago, he was the only one I couldn't get to evacuate. Fought off the whole inferno with his own hose. Wouldn't surprise me if he had a platoon's worth of claymores set up on his perimeter."

I gave her another moment to come clean. No luck. "And?"

Leslie went back on the offensive. "And what? That he was on the *Stryker*? And let me guess, you're in a tizzy 'cause I didn't tell you about him? Two words: you're welcome. He's a mean SOB, never wanted anything to do with this town *or* you. He belongs up there, not down here, where he could mess your head up even more."

CLICK.

Why was I always surprised?.

I hung up the phone and walked around the house, turning on every light, just like the good old bad days. Shivering, I turned up the thermostat and, after a few tries, it ignited. Flooded with light and heat, my small cottage glowed, ready to stand watch with me. At least for tonight.

Tomorrow, time for a house call on Liam Quinn.

Blackberry Cobbler

"Well, good morning to you too, Blanche." The gull's cranky squawk announced my arrival from her perch atop The Fog Cutter Café sign. Marco really needed to have someone get up there and clean that thing. By the looks of it, Blanche had been busy decorating it over the past few weeks. As the last of the morning breakfast crowd filtered out, I headed inside and sat at the counter.

Last night, I dug out a dog-eared Rand's Atlas and traced the route to Quinn's house. Set near the summit of Wolf Mountain at the end of a dirt logging road, his homestead would have a view of not just The Cove, but the entire coast, all the way to California. With a dozen or more switchbacks, it was at least a two-hour trip.

Sustenance was definitely needed— and a cobbler and coffee bribe. Although picking season ended months ago, Marco had canned the juiciest blackberries from Crescent City to Gold Beach. A Cutter specialty, his blackberry cobbler balanced sweetness and tartness perfectly. He baked the dough and filling together, but the topping is the secret: equal parts cookie and pie crust, dusted with sugar, pulled fresh from the oven. A half dozen every morning, never a day ahead. One bite and even a grumpy old mountain man couldn't resist.

The "new" owner (for the past fifteen years), Marco had inherited his father's personality: none. After making me wait for five minutes in his empty restaurant, he emerged from the kitchen. I pointed at the bakery display case.

"Need that last berry cobbler and a bear claw, to-go, please. Oh, and a cup of black coffee."

Marco grunted, but obeyed. He poured the coffee into a large Styrofoam cup and, before capping it, dropped in two plump blackberries. Even though he knew I took it black, he added a plastic stirrer. My cash sat untouched on the counter as he disappeared back into the kitchen.

Inexplicably, this small gesture moved me. As kids, Leslie and I had created our own special order: coffee with a dash of blackberry. When we sipped our signature Cutter coffee, we weren't stuck on Timberview Lane; we were strolling the Champs-Élysées. Call us gross; we didn't care. We reveled in it. Our tradition survived adolescence, marriages, even the owner's death. And now, the "Jen and Leslie Special" came automatic at the Cutter. A dash of humanity on a wet, unsteady morning.

I tossed an extra five on the counter, grabbed the pie, and dashed to my Bronco, head down, with Blanche's shrill cawing ringing in my ears.

Sole Survivor

He better be home.

I'd considered calling ahead. But, mysterious hill people don't have phones, now do they? Eva confirmed the last telephone pole on the mountain overlooked Beaver Creek Bridge, a good ten miles below Quinn's compound. I set aside the question of *How in the hell could she possibly know that?* and zeroed in on the mission at hand. Operation Contact Liam Quinn was underway.

It didn't take me two hours to get there. It took three. I managed fine until the pavement ended. Then the winter rains revealed their handiwork, turning the rutted logging road into Flanders Field with shell-sized potholes. Twice I had to stop to drag fallen branches out of my path. As I climbed higher, the road treacherously narrowed, daring me to continue.

During the ascent, I visualized Quinn's place. Best I could come up with was a shack straight out of *Deliverance*, similar to the rusted-out green-and-white trailer I'd passed five miles and four switchbacks ago. And please, no banjos, or I'm staying in the car.

I wasn't just wrong. I was spectacularly wrong.

No moss-covered fifth wheels or chained-up hound dogs here. Instead, I arrived at a gigantic, pristine two-story log cabin. Excuse me, *compound*, not cabin. The fortress overlooked Boyd's Cove with a sweeping view of the Pacific. Three riverstone chimneys dotted the roofline. A railed verandah encircled an endless wraparound porch. Massive beams of old-growth timber framed the porch, as majestic as Parthenon columns.

The place screamed movie star retreat in Coeur d'Alene, or maybe a retired oil exec in Boulder. An old hermit Navy hermit? Didn't see that coming.

Pretty sure old Liam wasn't seeing many visitors 'round these parts. How could I make contact without catching a bullet? I climbed out of the Bronco, slamming the door loudly to announce my presence. *I come in peace! Not trying to sneak up on anyone!*

I started up the slate path toward the porch, eyeing the elk-horn handles on the massive front door. The stone glistened, like it had been set yesterday.

"Lady, you must be very, very lost."

The voice cracked the air behind me. I spun, my hands shooting up like I was in some Saturday matinee stickup.

Ah, now *this* was more on script. To the rear of my truck stood a six-foot codger in overalls and red flannel, capped off with a beat-up AC Trucking hat. A brown lab, the muscle of the operation, sat at his feet, sizing me up.

But it was the enormous ax in his right hand that spun my compass. Quinn ran his thumb along the freshly-sharpened, beveled blade. My firewood ax back at the cottage got dusted off a few times a year. This one looked like an everyday companion.

He stepped closer. I retreated, hands still raised like I was staring down the Dalton Gang.

"Mr. Quinn, nice to meet you! I'm Genevieve Boyd, mayor of Boyd's Cove. I was also an ER nurse at Curry County

Hospital. I brought you coffee and cobbler! The coffee's a little cold, but it's right here in my truck. Let me grab it for you."

Taking his silence as permission, I plucked the goodies from the front seat. The lab was immediately interested, sniffing the pastry bag.

Quinn was not.

"Look, I don't know how you know me or why you're here, but the good news for me is I don't give a damn either way."

He lifted the cleaver off his shoulder and leaned on it like a cane.

"You wasted your time." He jabbed the ax toward the road like a pointer. "You and your cobbler need to get the hell out of here."

Eva was right so far about Citizen Quinn. People like him—those who end up on Wolf Mountain, or in The Cove—don't get there by accident. I'd dealt with plenty of them in the ER. Upon arrival (usually against their will), they're in full-blown bully mode. A thirty-minute wait to be seen? *No one here respects my time!* Fill out some paperwork? *I already did this at my doctor's office!* Their interactions with society only confirm it's an unholy inconvenience to be avoided beyond a couple Fred Meyer runs per year.

As you learned in grade school, a bully has to be stood up to. But, what if he's holding... an ax?

"Mr. Quinn, I'll be on my way, but I drove hours to meet you. Since you were on the *Stryker*, I just wanted to ask—"

That was as far as I got.

"That's why you're here?" he sputtered, the words tumbling over each other. "Get lost! I got nothing to say! Book writers, magazines, TV assholes have been bothering me for years! Just... leave my ass... alone!"

"But Mr. Quinn, I'm not—"

Now even the lab was glaring at me. Time was up. All my chips were needed at the center of the table right now.

"Look, I didn't mention I'm also the daughter of Captain Preston Boyd."

That got his attention. He examined me closely, like a suspect in a police line-up. Satisfied there was at least a possibility I was telling the truth, he leaned the ax against a nearby tree. He approached and took the tin of cobbler from my hand. After peering inside, he closed the lid.

"This stuff is the only reason to go anywhere near that goddamn town. If you're the mayor, no wonder it's such a hellhole."

Quinn turned and climbed the front steps of his porch. Arms crossed, he turned around to appraise me again.

"Look, here's some free advice worth what it costs you—nuthin'. The *Stryker* was forty f-in' years ago. Ancient history as far as I'm concerned. Keep it the hell out of your life too. Nothing to be gained by kickin' over tombstones. Some things should just stay gone."

As he vanished inside, I glimpsed an antler chandelier the size of a small tree. Dozens of elk prongs twisted and clicked together like giant Legos. Quinn must have slaughtered an entire herd for this masterpiece. The Barnacle regulars often wondered where all the elk had gone. Mystery solved.

I threw the Bronco into low gear and inched my way back down the mountain. Too bad I didn't get a chance to invite

Popeye to the *Stryker* festivities next week. Harry Reasoner would've loved him.

The Visitor

In grade school, you learned about the four seasons. Summer and winter kick off with their respective solstices; spring and fall wait patiently for their equinoxes. But there's another season in Boyd's Cove. A season unaffected by the declinations of the sun, lunar phases, or groundhog sightings. We locals have a name for it: "November Gloom."

What makes this time of year special? Nothing at all. And (as you've already figured out) that's the point. It's not Thanksgiving yet. Christmas hasn't snuck up on us. No holiday lights strung across Main Street, nothing to look forward to but endless gray skies and darkness by dinnertime. The tease of a rare sunny weekend is just that: a Mother Nature bait-and-switch swept away by the next gushing atmospheric river. Unlike its sibling seasons, November Gloom offers no promises or carrot sticks of good tidings to come.

Exhausted, I finally pulled into my muddy driveway. A fresh storm had escorted me down Wolf Mountain, snowballing in intensity as I got closer to the sea. Gloom showers were usually more of a mist, a drizzle that forces you to squint at the porch light to confirm it's really raining.

But not tonight. Forks of lightning sliced through the night sky, spotlighting a mix of just-before-the-tornado-touches-down hail and Oklahoma-sized raindrops. Both pelted me mercilessly as I splashed up my cottage steps.

The roar of the once-a-decade November thunderstorm subsided as I closed the door behind me. The pitch-black cabin shuddered under shockwaves from passing salvos of thunder, each artillery boom closer than the last. I flicked the living room light switch once, then twice. Nothing. How long had the power been out? Two years ago, Pacific Power had taken a week to send a tech out here. And that was during summer.

Can't worry about that now, though. Bigger fish to fry. Like a spastic strobe, erratic flashes of sheet lightning provided glimpses of illumination as I searched for my roommate.

"Reef, where are you, boy? Mama's home!" Though the pug usually met me at the front door, I wasn't worried. Over the years, he'd weathered his share of in-flight Oregon Coast turbulence, and aside from a couple of freaky howling episodes, he'd ridden out those squalls just fine.

Must be in the laundry room. The little bugger loved curling up in the laundry basket before I had a chance to put things away. I was headed there when I first heard the sound.

Cre-eak... SLAM! Cre-eak... SLAM!

First thought: it's outside—a shutter ripped loose by the gusting wind. But no. Too loud. Too close.

Cre-eak... SLAM! Cre-eak... SLAM!

Was it inside? *Oh my frickin' God!* I bolted toward the clatter at the back of the cottage.

Fuck! To my horror, my always-locked kitchen back door was flung wide open. A torrent of ocean-driven wind battered against the wooden frame, swinging and slamming it like an enraged teenager. Shards of shattered glass littered the rain-slick floor. I slipped, landing hard on one knee as the gale howled through the gaping doorway. Below, the ocean raged against the cliffs, the spray hissing and stinging as it lashed the cottage windows.

Panic time. No sign of my dog. *Where's my baby? He wouldn't have gone out the back door, would he?*

"Reef, where are you?" I shouted frantically. The door thrashed on its hinges, and as I rushed to close it, I slipped again, crashing onto the linoleum. Glass splinters bit into my palms, lodging like darts in a dartboard.

"Tsshhh-ah!" Through gritted teeth, I gingerly brushed off the shards, straining for any sign of Reef in the suffocating dark.

Later I'd tell myself I'd known it a split-second before. Call it intuition, call it precognition. Call it whatever. Like when you glance up from your hot dog a second before the blistering foul ball comes rocketing your way.

In any event, I looked up, and there he was: Seaman Hayes—R.I.P., figment of my imagination. In the flesh, towering over me.

Oh, and clutching a steel kitchen cleaver in his right hand.

Not real. Not possible. I was seeing things. *Just like the old days.*

But the figure didn't move. Didn't fade. Didn't vanish.

Reason lagged behind sight. My mind shook its head, refusing the evidence.

This wasn't memory or madness.

God help me, he was real.

My mouth opened, but my throat locked tight. A strangled rasp escaped anyway. Still on the floor, I shielded my face, bracing to wake up from this all-timer of a nightmare.

On the beach earlier, Hayes was a cadaver, lifeless as stone. Not now. His cheeks flushed pink, the seaman scanned the room as he stood motionless over me. Not a zombie from the movies. A person, as alive as you and me.

My body took the reins from my brain. I crab-walked backward, my hands crunching through glass, none of which I felt. When my back hit the wall, I dared to look up again.

Still in uniform, the teenager with tousled, jet-black hair and I locked eyes. Our connection, if there was one, lasted a fraction of a second. No words, no revelations. Just determination. A job to do. A mission, and some old lady wasn't going to stop him.

I found my voice, shrieking maniacally as he raised the blade overhead like a Tudor executioner.

WHOOSH!

Jesus Christ! A blast of air whisked past my cheek as the cleaver slashed into the drywall behind me. Whimpering and swearing, I lowcrawled to the other side of the kitchen, desperately groping for something—anything—to defend myself.

But Hayes ignored me. Instead of pulling the cleaver free, he began sawing into the cracked gypsum. Plaster dust and scraps of pink insulation rained down, coating the kitchen floor.

After a few strokes, Hayes balled his right hand into a fist, and cocked it behind him.

Oh my God!

He swung. The Frazier haymaker detonated against the wall, blasting powder and rubble across the room. I screamed again as a sickening crunch—bone? Drywall? I didn't know—echoed through the cottage.

That was quite enough for this lady.

Panting and wheezing, I stumbled out of the cabin into the night. My Bronco—my unkillable, rock-solid Bronco—awaited, a lifeboat out of this shitstorm. Staccato raindrops peppered its roof as I yanked open the door, fumbling for the spare key under the seat. I peeled out, ripping down the driveway.

Oh, shit!

Forgot something.

Reef!

But I couldn't just go back in there, could I? Van Helsing himself might sit this one out. I swallowed a sob, biting back a curse.

Nope, had to. Never forgive myself if something happened to that damn dog.

I forced my foot onto the brake, then slammed it down. The Bronco lurched forward.

I was going back in.

But I needed a weapon—something, anything. My hands rifled through the Bronco. Just a coffee mug and a half-eaten candy bar. Short-circuited, I fought to breathe, let alone think.

The rain had eased, slackening to a soft dance on the roof. I closed my eyes and buried my head in my hands.

Calm. Get calm. Stay calm. You can figure this out.

A few shaky breaths later, an idea hit: check the trunk, under the spare. I dug in the dark for the tire iron

Got it!

Like a cop at a Berkeley protest, I swung a few practice arcs through the air, feeling its weight. Jaw set, I marched toward the madhouse awaiting me inside.

Minus the distant symphony of the fading storm, the cottage was draped in black silence. Crowbar in hand, I nudged the door open.

CREEEKK...

The handle's rusty whine crackled through the dark like a gunshot in an empty alley. Wincing, my arm hit the wall phone and—*CRASH!*—the receiver skittered across the floor.

Might as well have rolled in with the Boyd's Cove marching band.

Shuffling through the darkness, I crept inside. The kitchen was licking its wounds from the melee. Water streaked across the floor, puddles pooling in uneven dips. Cabinet doors hung open, and broken glass and chunks of plaster littered the counters.

Where was Hayes?

Nowhere to be found. But someone else was.

A tiny, warm weight pressed against my leg,

"Reef! You scared the hell out of me!"

We collapsed to the floor and cried it out together. Kissing my face with slobbery devotion, he buried himself in my chest. His tail spun madly until the frenzy subsided and he sagged against me, spent.

But where was my uninvited guest?

Hayes's cleaver was where he'd left it, plunged into the obliterated kitchen wall. My mother's long-ago self-defense advice cut through: *They gotta think you're crazier than they are.*

Cavewoman logic: one weapon good, two weapons better. I threw open a kitchen drawer and seized the biggest knife I could find.

Tire iron in one hand, carving knife in the other, I went full Blackbeard, howling into the blackness:

"GET OUT! OUT OF MY HOUSE, MOTHERFUCKER! I'LL KILL YOU AGAIN, RIGHT HERE, RIGHT NOW!"

My mother's advice held true. Maybe it *is* possible to scare the dead away. With Reef at my heels, a furtive room-by-room, closet-by-closet search turned up nothing.

Seaman Hayes—or whatever it was—had vanished.

Exhausted, I stumbled back to the demolished kitchen. The back door to the beach steps was wide open, hanging by a single hinge. Invited in, the storm had tracked in a slick coating of rain and mud across the linoleum floor. Meanwhile, a soft, jazzy midnight drizzle, settled in to keep Reef and I company.

Now, finally, the madness of the last twenty-four hours split me open. Clutching myself, I crumpled to the floor, and let it all come—the fear, the rage, the grief. In jagged, heaving sobs, it poured out, years', decades' worth.

Regret.

Loss.

Grief I hadn't known I was carrying.

And then, like scales slipping from my eyes, an epiphany.

Unquestionably, these sorrows had forged the armor around my heart. But a new, unnerving emotion had seeped in too. A shocking truth, something I'd never, ever considered.

Guilt.

Guilt? For what? I'd been a good daughter. A good friend. Not perfect, but loyal, reliable.

What the hell do I have to feel guilty about?

Startled by the sound of my own voice, I laughed bitterly. Who was supposed to answer? Seaman frickin' Hayes? Reef?

And then, slowly, the answer took shape, so plain I wondered how I hadn't seen it before.

All my life choices—hiding behind my father's legacy, feeling shame for my mother, wasting years as a pathetic recluse—had one root, a single parent.

Cowardice.

Not fear of one thing.

Fear of *everything*.

Heroism isn't genetic. It's not inherited, like high blood pressure or a talent for hitting the sauce too hard. Unlike my father, I had never stood my ground. Not once. Just a piece of Cove flotsam, drifting in the current, waiting to wash up on some random shore.

A coward. Unworthy of sympathy. Incapable of grace.

Self-delivered truth bombs hit the hardest. This one was a stunner, like flashing blue lights in your rearview after saying yes to that third beer.

But this wasn't the time to drown in self-pity. I could drink myself numb over this mess later. I laid the crowbar on the counter and, as my rollercoaster brain skidded back into the station, I lifted the safety bar to rejoin the world.

The power was still out. I blinked, letting my eyes adjust to the darkness. I let out a low moan at the sight of my shattered kitchen.

Then I saw it, jutting from the wall.

Stryker's Ghost of Christmas Past had left behind a souvenir: my cleaver, buried to the hilt in faded starfish and seahorse wallpaper.

Despite a valiant effort, I was no King Arthur, and the blade wouldn't budge. Hayes must have found a stud. The lower section of the wall was demolished, a gaping hole where a rarely used telephone had once hung. I leaned closer, peering into the opening.

And there it was.

Plaster dust lingered in the air as I rubbed my eyes for a closer look. There, lodged beneath a collapsed beam, lay a small trunk.

The wall opening was too small to remove it, so I picked up where Hayes had left off, tearing down the remaining drywall, piece by piece. One final, furious kick, and the excavation was complete.

The size of a large jewelry case, the lid of the strongbox was secured with a thick leather band. Despite the darkness, the small chest looked familiar.

Yes, I knew this box! It had been in my parents' bedroom for years, atop the bureau dresser they shared.

What was it doing *here*, sealed inside this wall?

I shivered as I pieced it together. Hayes's rampage hadn't been random. He had been after this.

But why?

I fumbled through the kitchen junk drawer for a flashlight. A twist of the brass handle released the leather band, and the lid lifted.

No gold. No silver. No secret will. Instead, the box was stuffed with at least a hundred letters, neatly crammed together, side by side.

With a final peal of soft thunder, the storm retired for good, rolling off to the west. Holding the box, I glanced at the crowbar on the kitchen counter, and shook my head at the irony of it all.

Yes, I was still a coward. No doubt about that. And one flash of bravery to save a scaredy-cat pug doesn't merit a Silver Star or Distinguished Cross.

But... could it be a flicker of hope? A chance that, after forty-nine years of auditioning for the damsel's role, I might finally get to play the hero?

You've got to admit, there's some evidence. Just this once, in this one ridiculous, terrifying moment, I stood instead of cowering, stared instead of flinching. Maybe, just maybe, a spark of Preston Boyd courage had sneaked into my bones.

Probably not. Let's not get carried away. Chalk this evening up to the more likely explanation: temporary insanity. Really. What rational person would charge in to do battle with a cleaver-wielding demon from the afterlife armed with only a rusty old tire iron?

Don't mess with my pug.

Young Love

Some things can wait until morning: dishes in the sink, balancing the checkbook. Best to hold off at least til sunrise before I start celebrating the fact this fracas wasn't just another psychotic break.

The white-coats can see for themselves. Those aren't my prints on the knife in the wall. And the size-10 muddy bootprints by the fridge? Please. Jenny Boyd ain't crazy. At least not tonight.

But she's a curious cat. And she had a flashlight. What were these letters all about?

I slid the first envelope free. The stamp, postmarked "March 1, 1928," was foreign. Chinese? No... the rounded flower was a sakura. Japanese, definitely. The typed return address confirmed it.

Ms. Miyuki Yamacho
National Socialist Japanese Workers Party
Kanagawa Ward, Yokohama, Japan
The recipient?
Lieutenant Commander Preston Boyd,
Naval Operations
I knew almost nothing of my father's time in Japan before I was born. A few photographs survived from his four-year attaché posting in Kanagawa Prefecture. One sticks in my mind. The image is so faded and blurry that I couldn't make out his face—two black specks masquerade as his cobalt-blue eyes.

Yet even through the grain, Preston the man broke free of the frame. Half at attention beneath a torii gate, his cap set at a devil-may-care tilt, he radiated Roaring Twenties swagger. My mother was still five years away, waiting at a USO dance in Bremerton. His future was a blank page as he manned the helm of an uncharted life.

Ms. Yamacho's first letter on Japanese government stationery was remarkably dull. Finalizing details for some diplomatic party: ordering linen napkins, deciding who sits where... blah, blah, blah. Just two single-spaced pages of a meticulous to-do list.

Seaman Hayes needed me to see this?

On to the next letter, then the next, I alternated between Miyuki's carefully folded missives and Preston's replies. In all, they'd carried on a correspondence spanning thirteen years, ending abruptly in November '41, weeks before Pearl Harbor. Nothing if not consistent, these two pen pals. The longest gap? A few months in '36, right around the time I was born.

Guess Preston was a little busy then.

Six months in, the letters started to change. The official letterhead was replaced by an elegant rice-straw washi parchment. Both sides abandoned typewriters for quills, and I drew a deep breath as I recognized my father's exactingly precise cursive. Miyuki's English strokes grew bolder throughout the years, reflecting the soft, rounded curves of her native hiragana.

But the transformation wasn't confined to pen and paper. Their topics, once constrained to embassy updates and local politics, were inexorably crowded out by their real interest.

Each other.

Curled up on the couch with Reef asleep on my lap, I, letter by letter, met Ms. Miyuki Yamacho. The only daughter of a Japanese admiral, she had lost her mother as a child. Miyuki had accompanied her father on his liaison assignment to D.C., where she mastered English and studied at Georgetown. Back in Japan, she served as her father's unofficial aide-de-camp, and once recounted a night that could have been ripped from a thriller: hot-headed junior officers had stormed their home during a failed coup d'état, and her father, sidearm in hand, had faced them down.

I read on in disbelief as it became clear where this was headed. Within a year, they had unmoored from getting-to-know-each-other to fervent passion. Miyuki's prose was exquisitely beautiful. Page after page, year after year, she bared her heart to Preston as the world hurtled toward war.

"No night is so dark that our love cannot light the way to dawn."

"Your touch lingers on my skin like the warmth of a summer day."

I was right to be shocked, wasn't I? We all know (at least in theory) that our parents had lives before we popped onto the scene. But, c'mon—a six-foot-two naval officer who can waltz *and* foxtrot? He must have had a thousand other girls queued up for his dance card.

I knew the bachelor had *some* skills, but I let out a slow whistle as my father fully unleashed his inner Lord Byron. His return letters matched Miyuki's ardor line for line. Feast your eyes on these gems.

"Through the sighing wind, your voice echoes in my heart."

"Among a thousand ordinary stones, you are the one that sparkles."

OK, so maybe Keats doesn't need to lose any sleep. But let's acknowledge the officer's solid B+/A- level composition. Not bad for a taciturn sailor whose literary background consisted of writing efficiency reports and ration requisitions.

My mood darkened as I reached the middle of the stack. Despite Preston's redeployment to America, marriage, and the birth of a new (gorgeous) daughter, their affair continued. Not physically, of course. But 5,000 miles of ocean couldn't snuff out the wildfire lit all those years ago. I cringed as I thought of my poor mother. Had she known she was emotionally sharing him, heart and soul, with a young, untouchable love? A mistress who would never age, never nag, never disappoint?

The brightness of the Oregon dawn finally reached a tipping point, and I turned off the flashlight. Only two letters left. And I was wrong. Pearl Harbor wasn't the cut-off after all.

The last two had been sent in '42, almost a year later. The first, dated October 2, was from Miyuki, addressed to a P.O. Box in town my father had been using for years.

No sonnets or pleasantries in this one. Something far more urgent.

Dear Preston - all the arrangements have been made. My father is ready. The Murakumo will rendezvous at the agreed upon coordinates on November 1. I've included every precious letter of our past correspondence in this mailing. See you soon, my love.

And then the final letter, the last one my father would ever write. On my seventh birthday, October 14, 1942.

Tell the Admiral I wish him calm seas. Until we meet again.

My seas were no longer calm. A tryst. A double life. And personal contact with the enemy. For the first time, I grasped the motive for Seaman Hayes barging into my life. The most ancient, galvanizing motivation of all.

Revenge.

A Cowboy Versailles

It's nice to have a guy.

A guy at the Pontiac dealership so you don't get skinned alive. A guy at the hospital who makes sure your aunt with COPD gets the room where the radiator works. A guy who can fix stuff and not blab about it.

Gus Sawyer was my guy. Yesterday, I'd called in a favor with Boyd Cove's one-and-only handyman, who'd kindly shaken off his daily hangover and come right over (He'd crushed on me in high school, and you know how sticky those memories can be). I kept his coffee topped off while he hung drywall, replaced the back door, and wondered why he hadn't been invited to the wild frat party in my kitchen. For the bargain price of only two hundred bucks and yet another rerun of the senior year glory stories I'd heard at The Barnacle a hundred times, my cottage was back in one piece.

Funny how the road up Wolf Mountain felt shorter when I had a score to settle. Bouncing through potholes, I hogged the middle lane as I raced toward the summit. Reef had the good sense to sit this one out, and was holding down the couch at home behind Gus's brand-new double locks.

No coffee or cobbler treats this time. Liam Quinn and I had unfinished business.

Gravel spat from my Bronco's tires as I swung into his driveway. Quinn sat on the porch, coffee in hand, gazing out over his trillion-dollar view.

This time, I caught the bastard by surprise. Too late for him to grab his shotgun or scary dog. The codger hadn't bothered to change clothes, still sporting the same loose-hanging, dusty overalls as last time.

Shaking his head, he spat on the ground and bared his teeth, a hillbilly silverback ready for combat. But I wasn't about to be out-alphaed this time. I'd seen combat of my own. Go ahead, beat your chest till it bruises, old man. You're riddled with hypertension, hyperlipidemia, every "hyper" in the index of my nursing textbooks. Your time's up, and everyone knows it. Everyone but you.

"OK, Quinn. No more bullshit. I've had a long, long couple of days, and I'd rather clean out my septic tank with my bare hands than drive up here again. But here I am. 'Cause you owe it to Seaman Hayes and every man on the *Stryker* to tell me the truth. The *whole* f-ing truth about what happened that night."

Roiled, Quinn hesitated. But a hyena doesn't surrender his scavenged gazelle kill without a fight. He quickly centered himself and waved me off.

"Lady, I told you once already, so consider yourself warned. Get the hell off my property and leave me alone!" He jerked his thumb toward a newly-tacked sign on a fir tree:

No Trespassing—If You Can Read This You're in Range.

Nope. Not having it.

"Oh, great, Liam. Made that just for me, huh? Guess you knew I'd be back. Now let's start over. No doubt, you did the world a favor by slithering up here and hiding like a weasel for all these years. But since you have no sense of duty to your fellow crewmates and weren't man enough to deal with this years ago when you had all your teeth, I guess it's up to me."

I paused and crossed my arms.

"Now pay attention. I found some letters between my father and a Ms. Miyuki Yamacho from Yokohama. When my father was a military attaché in Japan, they had an affair that continued after he returned home. They even made plans to meet during the war. Now, I need to know *exactly* what happened the night the *Stryker* went down."

"GRRR...GRRR... GRRR!"

Encroaching from the treeline, Quinn's lab was late to our party, but needed no prompts to remember how much it hated me. Snarling and snapping its jaws, it crouched low like a coiled spring, calculating if it should close the twenty yards between us.

Decision made.

The beast launched. Paws barely touching the ground, it hurtled toward me, a blur of fur and teeth.

With no good options, I took the only one I had.

I held my ground.

Oregon Cujo was only a heartbeat away when Quinn's hand shot up. Instantly, the lab stopped mid-leap, its feet digging into the dirt.

"Sit, Ranger. Sit."

The retriever dropped at Quinn's feet and relaxed. But the wagging tail and good-natured panting didn't chill me out. He had gone from Hyde to Jekyll in the snap of a finger. Ranger—the real silverback here— was waiting, just waiting, for the tiniest signal to finish what he had started.

The job of ripping me apart.

Quinn was silent. Then, to my surprise, he started to chuckle, rubbing his chin.

"You think you're so fucking smart. You don't know nuthin' about that night."

Time for the good cop approach.

"OK, then. Why don't you tell me?"

Quinn saw right through my amateur detective nonsense. His eyes narrowed, sharp and cold.

"Who are you, Perry Mason now? I don't have to tell you squat."

Unlike my last visit, it was a sunny day, and I took a hard look at the old cretin. Tall but too thin, the straps of his overalls threatened to slip off his bony shoulders. His steel-toed work boots were unlaced and caked with Wolf Mountain mud. His eyes had that gray, glassy tinge you see in the deeply aged, their colors faded like a mural too long in the sun. An angry rash crept up the side of his neck, stopping just below his chin.

In short, he looked terrible.

"Something's wrong. You're sick, aren't you?"

His reaction confirmed my diagnosis.

"So now you're a doctor? My lucky goddamn day. What you need to do is mind your business and get the hell out of here."

He turned and began climbing the steps of the sweeping front porch, leaning heavily on the handrail. Ranger followed anxiously behind, his demeanor shifted from psychopathic assassin to nervous caregiver.

Sorry, old boy. Nothing I—or the entire Mayo Clinic—could do to help here.

Out of breath and exhausted, Quinn collapsed into the nearest deck chair with a weary croak, that same grunt your father makes when he drags himself up from the couch after his third nap.

I climbed the porch stairs and sat on the top step. On this clear, sunny day, the view was transcendent. With a little imagination, you could see the curve of the earth meet the impossibly blue sky. Thin clouds stretched overhead like a faint fresco on an invisible ceiling. Evergreens carpeted the mountains all the way down to the sea.

The old hermit might have lacked social skills, but he'd built himself a Northwest Versailles, cowboy-style.

And he sure knew how to train a dog.

A few moments passed in silence. The retriever curled around Quinn's feet and lost interest in me. The cool, steady breeze helped me collect my thoughts.

"A nurse actually, not a doctor."

I wasn't sure he heard me.

"You're right. I'm not a doctor, but I *am* a nurse. And I know cancer when I see it."

Still no reaction. The bulge on his neck hinted at the lymphoma rocketing through his bloodstream, picking off organs one by one. Ranger moved aside as Quinn started to rock gently in the chair and looked out across the expanse.

Patience, Jenny, patience. He's got to come to you. It's the only way.

"Jesus Christ, you're worse than the damn cancer. If I didn't already have it, I'd be praying to catch it after five minutes of listening to your bullshit."

Quinn looked at me and chuckled darkly. "You're going to wish you had cancer after you hear this little yarn."

Here goes.

"OK, lady, you're asking about Foster Hayes. Yeah, Hayes was my bunkmate. We both specialized in radio comms, so we were on the bridge a lot. We were stuck on some stupid patrol up and down the West Coast that night, and hadn't seen port in weeks. I was dead-ass tired, just off a twelve-hour watch. Hayes and I rotated through the same bunk, so I woke his ass up for his shift and crawled into the rack.

"Maybe five minutes later, the asshole's shaking me awake." Quinn leaned forward, eyes bright. "Liam! Liam! Wake the hell up! I'm half-asleep, but he starts rambling about intercepting a message between the captain and a Japanese ship. For some goddamned reason, he thinks Boyd is planning to hand over the sub!"

Bile surged in the back of my throat, one of those secret, fake barfs you clamp down before it reaches the puke stage. Quinn didn't notice my watery eyes or horrified expression. He was too busy rewinding the tape on a forty-year-old nightmare.

"Told him he was full of it, but he wouldn't let it go. Then— and I can still hear him say this— he told me, 'Look, just park yourself topside by the hatch, at 2300 hours tonight. If I'm wrong, no big deal. But just be there.'"

He continued.

"So I say yes, just to get the dumbass off my back. At 2300, I headed up top. Sure as hell, maybe five minutes later, there's a huge commotion on the bridge. Alarms blaring, people screaming."

Quinn paused and closed his eyes.

"Hayes always had that Bowie knife on him. Not sure, but I think he decided to take matters into his own hands. Take out the captain himself. Things must have gotten messy, wrong lever, wrong switch, I don't know. Then, BAM! The whole frickin' sub pitches forward, nose-dives, straight down. Lights go out. It's pitch black, freezing water everywhere."

"And you escaped because you were stationed up top?" I pressed.

"That's right."

Now I was the one who needed a break. My worst suspicions were confirmed. My father wasn't John Paul Jones; he was Benedict Arnold, responsible for the death of his entire crew.

What happened next?" I asked.

"A fucking shitshow. I already had my life preserver on, or I wouldn't have lasted five minutes."

Quinn shuddered and looked past me, out toward the Pacific.

"Quietest night of my life. Just me, bobbing up and down in the dark like a cork. Full moon, so yeah, there was some light. Water was calm. But cold. Jesus... like a bucket of ice. Coldest I've ever been. Thought my bones would crack."

I shivered, imagining that freezing water. Waves like sledgehammers, and a cold that steals your teeth. Nothing's tougher than cancer. Except maybe this son of a bitch.

"Last thing I saw was what must have been a Japanese ship. Big bastard, coming right at me. Thought I was done. But somehow, it missed. Just slid past my dumb ass and hightailed it back to Tokyo."

He closed his eyes

"And that was it. Lights out for old Quinn. Next thing I know, I'm soaking in a steaming tub, cozy as Christmas. Drank the best cup of coffee I've had to this day."

"What happened? How'd you get there?"

Quinn grimaced.

"I ended up the uninvited guest of George Watson. Didn't know he was the town cop back then. Found me on the beach, more dead than alive. At least that's what he claimed. Dragged my sorry ass to his place, shoved me in a hot bath, and nearly crapped himself when I didn't croak. Came back to life like Frankenstein."

He looked at me for the first time since I'd sat down. "I'm hard to kill, in case you missed it."

I sucked in a breath. Officer George Watson. Sheriff Leslie's dad. Dead at least ten years now.

I've suffered betrayals in my life. We all have. And I've betrayed others. Just ask my ex. But this... this was next level.

Leslie, *mi mejor amiga*, Huckleberry to my Tom, had been lying to me every damn day of my life. She'd known the entire time and played along. A sin not just of omission, but of commission. Every day, every minute we'd spent together... a lie. A decades-long deception.

I was alone. I'd always been alone.

"I know. Unbelievable, right?" Quinn licked his lips, savoring his reclaiming of the upper hand. "Now, I already know what you're gonna ask next, honey-bunch. You're gonna wanna know why I kept this whole clusterfuck under wraps all these years, aren't you? Why didn't I just rat your Judas father out to the whole world right then and there?"

I couldn't give him the satisfaction.

"Actually, Quinn, the answer to that is obvious. So obvious, even a moron like you could figure it out."

I laid out my theory.

"Stop me if I go off the rails here. It's 1942. Pre-Midway, the high-water mark for the Empire of the Rising Sun. The Japanese have already picked out landing sites for their West Coast invasion. It's chaos: blackouts, air-raid sirens, militias forming. For the locals, it's the end of the world. And now, a decorated American naval officer tries to hand over his sub to the enemy, right at our doorstep?"

Picture painted, I moved in for the kill.

"No way. No way in the name of God and all things holy, can the Great American Public learn about this. Avoid panic at all costs. So, let me guess. Some Navy honchos show up, give you the 'for the sake of national security' speech. And for forty years, the story holds. The sacrifice of the brave American sailor. A strategy straight out of *Mein Kampf*—the bigger the lie, the more likely it'll be believed."

I was pretty sure I'd lost the geezer with my *Mein Kampf* reference. So, I asked the next logical question aloud.

"But why would a young Quinn go along with any of this? I'm sure you were as big an asshole then as you are now. A tin medal or two wasn't going to buy your silence."

I stood up, dusted myself off, and caught my reflection in the massive bay window running the length of the porch. Behind the glass, a polished redwood bar anchored the parlor with four saddlebar stools. Whiskey bottles filled the shelves behind the bar, staggered like bleachers in a baseball park. Gold cigarette stands flanked both card tables, and a silver spittoon tucked into one corner. Topped off with a floor-to-ceiling mirror from Virginia City, Quinn had recreated his own Wild West saloon, down to the finest detail.

The cowboy Disneyland clicked the next piece in place for me.

"Yeah, too bad Foster Hayes never got to sip bourbon here, Mr. Quinn." I sank back onto the step, striking my best Rodin Thinker pose. "Hmm... I wonder. How could an illiterate ass like you afford to build your own redneck Shangri-La way up here?"

I paused, stroking my chin for effect.

"I'm no Sherlock Holmes. Hell, I'm not even Dr. Watson. But I'll wager a guess or two."

My filibuster was over.

"A medal or two? Are you kidding me? Try a chestful!" he roared, slapping his hand over his heart. "I could've had more fruit salad than old Halsey himself! They wanted to gussy me all up and parade me around the country like a turkey to sell war bonds."

"But that's not what *you* wanted, is it?"

"Hell no! Why would I want any of that BS? I just wanted the hell out of the Navy, period."

I'd stuck the landing. "But that's not all, is it?"

Quinn wagged his finger furiously at me as he wound himself up.

"You're goddamn right it's not! If I'm going to keep their dirty little secret, the bastards are gonna pay. I wrote it all down for the suits so they couldn't screw it up: a full master chief's pension. Fifty grand, cash. That was a shit-ton of money forty years ago."

He grabbed the sides of the rocking chair and staggered to his feet.

"And the most important thing of all..."

Leaning on the back of the chair, he swept an arm wide, like some emeritus matador who'd danced with one bull too many.

"This land... as a kid, I hunted all of Noah's ark up here. Deer, beaver, even a bighorn sheep now and then. Gettin' me up here's good for them, too. They get me out of town, and don't have to worry about me blabbing sea stories after a few pints."

I'd heard enough. But old Quinn wasn't done.

"You know what the best part was? When I heard they named the town after your dickhead old man. Aye, aye, sir—that was something else. You said something about 'the bigger the lie'? Well, guess what, sweet cheeks? I wasn't the only Boyd's Cover keeping this trash buried. Why don't you high-tail it back down to The Barnacle and ask some of the other old-timers about the *Stryker*? Wish I could be there to watch them crap their pants."

You know what? I just might do that.

Best Friends

Sheriff Leslie held up her empty mug and gave it a pointed shake. The semi-new Cutter waitress—we still hadn't bothered to learn her name—had figured out how things worked around here. She beelined to our corner booth and poured us each a cup of hours-old coffee, black, no sugar. And, thankfully, no chit-chat.

Except for us, the café was empty, napping through the mid-afternoon doldrums before the dinner crowd. Pork chops and peas tonight, the most special of all the specials.

As always, Leslie didn't sip her coffee (or her beer, for that matter). She drank it. Four or five swigs, and the oversized mug was empty. More of a sipper myself, it took a couple of refills to get her up to speed on my recent adventures. She listened without interrupting.

Naturally, I buried the lead. In this case, *I found some old letters in the back of a closet* would have to suffice. Best to leave out the part where a raging ghost destroyed my kitchen, right?

As I rehashed my run-in with the *Stryker's* sole survivor, Leslie's eyes widened as she realized her forty-year cover was blown. She grimaced, nodding when I described her good samaritan father dragging Quinn off the beach and back to their house. She'd have been my age at the time, maybe eight. Just a kid

I'm no professional CIA interrogator, but it only took one open-ended question to buckle the knees of my law enforcement friend.

"So, the last thing the bastard yells to me as I'm getting into my truck is, 'Ask the old-timers about the *Stryker.*' What do you suppose he meant by that? Or is he just batshit?"

No more f-ing around. She knew I knew. Time to see everyone's hand, no folding allowed. Righteous, electric fury, the most dangerous kind, surged through me. I bit my lip and chose my next words carefully, the same ones I'd rehearsed with Reef over breakfast.

"Leslie, you've known all this since the day my father died. And yet—*and yet!*—you let me believe a lie, let me *live* a lie my entire life."

I leaned back, studying her stone-faced reaction. As they say in the artillery, when the target is perfectly triangulated and it's time to let loose the barrage: fire for effect.

I twisted the knife hard, hissing, "And why? For what? You on the take too, just like old Quinn?"

"Another cup, Sheriff?" The waitress appeared nervously over my shoulder, holding up a coffee pot.

Leslie blinked, and placed her hand on top of her mug, holding it there without breaking eye contact. Message received. The waitress beat a hasty retreat to the kitchen as my cross-examination continued.

"So, you knew... you knew from the..."

I couldn't say it out loud. My rage had given me the courage to confront my only friend. Now, it melted away, replaced by wrenching despair. Death and lies, that was my life. Balling up a napkin in my right hand, I surrendered to the grief, and started to sob.

Leslie patted my hand, then stood and walked toward the door. For a moment, I thought she was leaving... but no. Instead, she flipped the sign on the door to *CLOSED* and drew the blinds. No after-school shakes at the Fog Cutter today.

"All right. You want answers." Leslie sat back down and reached for her coffee mug. It was empty, so she pushed it away.

"I was home that night when my dad brought Quinn into the house. Actually, into my room. Into my bed."

Leslie closed her eyes and sighed.

"Daddy, of course, kicked me out, but I could hear everything through the heater vent. He called Dr. Chartel and Mayor Livingston, and they came over."

She was half-whispering now.

"I remember thinking wow, this is the first dead body I've ever seen. What else...I was sad 'cause the boy was just a teenager. Oh, and his fingernails were blue. The doctor put a finger by his nose to see if he was still breathing. A lot of yelling. Finally, a hot bath and some more chest compressions brought him back to life. He threw up water... so much frickin' water, I couldn't believe it. And then, right away he starts cursing out your father, raving that he's a traitor, that this was all his fault. Finally, he passed out and they put him back in my room."

Leslie rubbed her forehead like a genie's lamp, trying to summon up what happened next.

"I haven't thought about this in a long time, but I do know it was the mayor's idea to call the Navy. This was too big, too heavy, I remember hearing him say, for us to get involved."

A pained smile crossed Leslie's face.

"In the hours before my dad died, I actually had my own come-to-Jesus talk with him about that night. So here you go, straight from the horse's mouth. He told me that the next morning, while I was at school, two Navy officers, dressed in civilian clothes, met with my father, the mayor, and the doctor at his office.

"Bottom line, they insisted that Quinn was a liar, a malcontent with 'authority issues.'" However—their words, according to my father—'rumors can kill,' so this was a top secret situation. The story was set. The *Stryker* was sunk by the Japanese, not some renegade American captain."

Leslie took a deep breath and exhaled.

"So far, your standard run-of-the-mill shitty government cover-up. But then it got next-level evil. Our town leaders, my father included, decided to get clever. 'We have a condition,' they said, 'if you want us to keep our mouths shut.' The Navy was building a new base forty miles south of town. The plans included a new four-lane highway to run all the way down the coast to San Francisco."

Leslie signaled for more coffee, forgetting she had already closed the place. With a sigh, she continued.

"Their terms? Move the road east, about half a mile, for this stretch of the coast. Don't announce it yet... give their little troika a chance to buy up property around the exit ramps. And they'll take one of the worst military scandals in American history with them to their graves."

My despair ripened into all-out disgust. Misguided as they were, at least my father's actions were motivated by love, not by a handful of gas stations on the edge of the continent.

Leslie met me where I was.

"So they bought a bunch of worthless land and sold it to Shell, and later to McDonald's, for a small fortune. Those ponies of mine we used to ride? Paid for by the USS *Stryker*."

It had all been a game. From the Peppermint Forest to Gloppy Gulch, I'd been shuffled around the board by unseen players. Including Leslie Watson.

"Not that this matters," she continued. "But as you know, I moved out of my childhood home after my father died. Sold it all: the ponies, the RV. The ASPCA got a generous, anonymous donation I'm sure they're still talking about."

I scoffed, shaking my head.

"Great. You cleansed your soul. No time in Purgatory for you. But somehow, you couldn't quite bring yourself to let your childhood friend in on your little secret."

Silence. Leslie drummed her fingers on the Formica table, ending with two sharp raps on the booth paneling.

"And you want to know why? Why didn't I tell you?"

Done with all this, I started to get up.

"At this point, it's your business, not mine. I'm not gonna beg. If you want to tell me, go ahead. If not, leave me the hell alone."

She cleared her throat. "All right Jenny... here goes."

"My decision goes back, way back... all the way to the beginning, to that first night I slept on the sofa while Quinn was in my room. I remember thinking I should hop on my Schwinn first thing in the morning, find Jenny, and spill my guts."

I remembered that bike. Blue, with a horn on the handlebar.

She continued.

"I stared at the ceiling all night. Didn't even close my eyes. And I asked myself a question: if the shoe was on the other foot... would I want to know? If I had a father I worshiped—and I've never met anyone more convinced her father was Jesus Christ himself than you—would I want to know, hours after his death, that he was a fucking traitor? That he betrayed everyone? Betrayed me?"

She shook her head.

"That was a hard no for me. So there you go. Good intentions, crappy result, but that was my thinking, and it held up for forty years."

And then the dreaded words. "And that's not all."

Leslie hesitated before emptying the vault.

"Remember your birthday, the ceremony in front of the town hall?"

"To be honest, yes and no."

Some hazy snippets lingered from that day. It was a Saturday. My sweet sixteenth had been dubbed "Preston Boyd Day," and the town square was packed. A podium had been erected in front of a monument to the *Stryker* heroes, their names etched into the gray marble. With only two misery-filled years left to live, my mother sat in the front row on folding chairs borrowed from the Elks lodge. It was spring, and her allergies were in full bloom.

To stave off the inevitable boredom, I'd tucked a paperback copy of *Sense and Sensibility* in my handbag. Halfway through the ceremony, just as I reached for it, my name was called: "Miss Genevieve Boyd, daughter of Captain Preston Boyd, please join us on stage." Stunned, I took off my reading glasses and headed toward the microphone, prodded by Leslie, who was sitting next to me.

Here's where it got fuzzy. I was shooed onto the stage and stood before the crowd like a heifer at auction, basking in glories that weren't mine. The mayor rhapsodized, overusing words like *valor* and *sacrifice*, presenting me as Exhibit A—physical proof that noble gladiators like Preston had once existed, a living reminder for people to show their gratitude.

Familiar with the *Stryker* saga, the townspeople listened respectfully. I pretended to pay attention, listening for cues the address was wrapping up. Suddenly, the crowd erupted, leaping to its feet. The applause was genuine and earnest, palms smashing together as if a pennant had been won. The speaker seized my hand, softly at first, then so vigorously he needed both to convey his enthusiasm. Instinctively, I gave a small wave to the crowd, lip-synced a few thank-yous, and retreated to my seat.

Once the honor guard had retired the colors.Leslie filled me in. The good people of Boyd's Cove had just footed my future college tuition!

Good news for me? Of course. College was not on any of the channels I was watching. For the first time, I glimpsed a future beyond slinging hash browns at The Fog Cutter.

My appreciation grew as I realized the enormity of the sacrifice. There were no Safeways with fresh arugula or German car dealerships in Boyd's Cove. The town—a hard-scrabble lot who left their storm windows up late into spring to keep the thermostat low—had pitched in to help an awkward teenager too shy to even say "hi" on the street.

Winning the college lottery was also, in a way, a release for my mother. It gave her the final necessary permission she needed to end her life. Does she take that midnight walk into the surf toward Forget Me Knot rock without knowing I'm provided for?

Unknowable. But I'd like to think not.

Leslie was a mob movie buff, and I recognized the bones of her opener.

"Yeah, well, since we're taking care of all our business at once here, there's one more thing you gotta know. It wasn't the townspeople who paid off your college."

"Huh?"

"Nope... anchors aweigh—it was our U.S. Navy friends once again to the rescue."

She elaborated.

"My father may have been a shit in some ways, but he knew how to pull off a proper shakedown. He told the ice cream suits that your sixteenth birthday was"—Leslie crooked two fingers in the air—"'an opportunity to honor the legacy of an American hero.' So, look on the bright side: the Navy paid for your education, and you never had to serve a day in uniform."

There was a bright side? Up was down. Black was white. The lies were so bold, so deeply embedded, they were stitched into every seam of my life. I reached across the table and grabbed both of her hands. For the first time—hell, maybe *ever*—I saw Leslie's eyes brimming with tears.

"I'm sorry, Jenny, I'm just... fucking sorry."

I pulled her closer across the table until our foreheads touched. I gave her hands a final hard squeeze and let go.

Sucker-punched, a muffled, "It's all good now," was all I could muster.

Learning these secrets had been a shock. But as Hitchcock says, you create suspense by making sure the audience sees it coming. Leslie wasn't stupid. There were too many loose ends for this to go on forever. She'd spent decades knowing a monster waited at the end of the hallway, and a reckoning was due. The cover-up is always more exhausting than the crime.

Maybe I was wrong. Perhaps there was a bright side after all. Dragging these secrets into the light meant freedom not just for me, but for her.

But not just yet. I still needed one more thing.

"OK girl, you want to take care of all the Boyd family business tonight? I need a favor. And I need it now."

Boyd's Cove's finest straightened up. A clanging from outside interrupted our tête-à-tête, courtesy of a hungry patron chasing The Cutter's early bird special. Apparently, the "CLOSED" sign was meant for everyone but him. Sorry, dude: your ham and scalloped potatoes would have to wait.

"Leslie, I can't stop now. What about her?"

Like she always did, she got me right away.

"Margaret."

I nodded. She reached across the table to hold my hands. They were calloused, with chipped, bitten nails.

"Jenny, I didn't come clean about your father. But I swear to f-ing God I don't know anything more about what happened to your mother. All I know is she left Evergreen, seemed to be fine, and then..."

"Yeah. And then. Glad you mentioned Evergreen. 'Cause that's exactly what I need help with."

Fog
Cutter

No More Heart to Break

Sanitarium. Asylum. Are there two more terrifying words in the English language?

A decade ago, the Evergreen Sanitarium was progressively renamed the Evergreen Convalescent Home. To be fair, it was a huge improvement over Evergreen Lunatic Asylum, its moniker when I was a child. The "Home" sat on prime cliffside real estate just south of town, a few miles from the California border.

Remarkably undiscovered by the Wes Cravens of Hollywood, it could've been a plug-and-play set for a horror film. It was a cinematographer's dream: enter through black iron gates and cross the manicured lawn dotted with croquet poles. Beneath a brooding sky, an orderly greets you at the hospital's Gothic doors to escort you to Registration. The hallways reek of Lysol and *Pseudomonas*. During visits to see my mother, I'd imagine how chilling this place must be at night, after lights-out and bed checks when the corridors went quiet.

Think you could handle it? Maybe... if this last fun fact doesn't bother you. The grounds had their own cemetery next to the patients' (prisoners'?) vegetable garden. I'd watch them hoeing away amidst the moss-covered headstones, waiting to be planted themselves.

Other than the name on the entrance sign, nothing much had changed since my teenage visits in the early '50s. A perky nurse-in-training shepherded me to the administrative wing and then down to the basement. There it was, last room on the left: *Medical Records*.

Public or private, bureaucracy's the same everywhere. Procedures abound, CYA rules that allow everyone to blame screw-ups on the system instead of themselves. Check-in protocols weren't much different from your average GP's office, other than the metal cagework separating the customers from the clerks. Half the fluorescent tubes overhead were dead; the rest buzzed and flickered. Shelves groaned under cardboard boxes of files, stretching toward the back like a police evidence cellar. And I was the gumshoe, on scene to investigate a particularly grotesque unsolved murder.

Not too far from the truth, actually.

"Ms. Genevieve Boyd. I have an appointment."

Welcome to Medical Records: the last stop before forced retirement. The clerk looked about the same age as my mother would've been during her final days at Evergreen. He glanced up from behind the grill and leaned back in his chair. White hair shot out wildly from underneath his newsboy cap, a token of rebellion against the many unkind years. Bleach could no longer rescue his yellowed orderly blouse from the cigarette smoke and all-day-long bottomless cups of coffee.

In violation of at least five hospital regulations, a portable microwave behind him beeped. Lunch—or was it early dinner?—was ready. Our transaction would have to wait.

Actually, no it wouldn't.

"Hold up. Before you dig into that Stouffer's lasagna—or whatever the hell that is—I'm here for the file on Margaret Boyd."

All the exhaustion and betrayal of the last few days had a perk: since everything was a lie anyway, I had stopped pretending. My new superpower was thrilling: I would simply say exactly what I was thinking. No fear, no judgment, no give-a-shit.

I found that telling the truth was like a loaded gun: it got results fast.

"All right lady, hold your horses. I got it right here."

He opened a desk drawer and held up a thick manila folder. "Need to sign for it."

Like a bank teller, he slid the folder and clipboard through the cage opening. A sticky note was attached: *Urgent, for Ms. G. Boyd. Authorized by Ofc. L. Watson.* I initialed the sign-out sheet and passed it back without a word.

"I'll need that back by close of business."

Yeah, right. You kept her here far too long already. Let's see what the State has to say about Mom.

By the end, my mother and I were perfect roommates. Courteous and dutiful, but distant. But it hadn't always been that way.

Prior to my father's death, her soft green eyes smiled easily. My father would tease that only lizards and spiders had green eyes. Once he had me aghast, he'd double down, wondering aloud if maybe Mom really was a lizard in human form.

Check her arms for scales! Her feet seem a little webbed, don't they? She'd laugh along and finally reel him in before I completely lost it.

Early on, in the maelstrom following my father's death, my mother bent but didn't break. During that first endless winter, the town rallied around us. Help arrived quietly and respectfully, always from the shadows. A smorgasbord of food appeared on our porch each day. Leslie must have spread the word that pie was my favorite dessert, because one day, half a dozen double-crust tarts—chiffon, pumpkin, cherry—paid us a visit. Our side fence, shredded by the wind, mysteriously repaired itself. Surely, these fine people were worthy of the sacrifice of my father and his men. My mother and I turned to each other for comfort, sharing her bed with the curtains drawn so I wouldn't have to look at the dark sea outside.

I staked out a depressing corner table in the empty hospital canteen. Picture the plastic trays and aproned lunch ladies from your school cafeteria minus the joy and bustle of actual children. Fortified with a twenty-five cent cup of watery coffee, I opened Margaret Boyd's file. The earliest doctor notes described my mother's state of mind a few months after that terrible November morning when the *Stryker* was lost.

January 21, 1943: Margaret Boyd, aged 33 years: Since the death of her husband in November, 1942, Ms. Boyd reports experiencing depressed mood and general lethargy. Specific symptoms include disinterest in eating, extreme fatigue and feelings of worthlessness. Diagnosis is melancholia, severe at times, but consistent with clinical grief. Prescribe rest and a three month course of Spirobarbital for sedative purposes.

A year later, the spiral had begun.

December 1, 1944: Patient showing signs of mental deterioration, triggered by the anniversary of the family tragedy. She alternates between manic and depressive states. Reports sleeping only 3-4 hours per night despite sedatives. Detected alcohol on patient's breath during appointment, but denied use. Increased dose of Spirobarbital, but warned patient not to combine with alcohol. Reports few social contacts, greater isolation.

I guess my mother didn't take kindly to what the doctors had to say that day. The next entry doesn't appear until nearly three years later.

November 28, 1947: *Patient seen on emergency basis, escorted by neighbor. Physical appearance consistent with excessive alcohol consumption: sallow, jaundiced skin, reddish tinge in cheeks and nose, a twenty pound weight loss since previous visit, numbness in hands and feet. Disheveled appearance. Poor nutrition.*

The next paragraph sent a chill up my spine.

Signs of early schizophrenia. Reports seeing imaginary people and objects. Claimed she witnessed her deceased husband's submarine circling Boyd's Cove and signaling her with flashing lights. Having intense nightmares with similar patterns. Reports dreaming she is in the submarine as it is sinking. Crew is in panic, screaming, crying. She's trampled by desperate sailors as icy water engulfs them all.

Ms. Boyd is mother to a thirteen year old daughter. If symptoms continue to worsen, the child's welfare must be considered.

Similar case notes chronicled her next few years of terrifying hallucinations and deepening despair.

Then, the final entry.

November 23, 1953: *Ms. Boyd is at serious risk of self-harm. Involuntary institutionalization recommended. During low tide, patient walked out to Forget Me Knot rock in Boyd's Cove wearing only a nightdress. Discovered by a neighbor, she resisted* *all attempts to retrieve her and law enforcement assistance was required. She was transported to Hospital against her will.*

It is clear her disease has progressed significantly. She now reports seeing and interacting with a member of the USS Stryker crew at different locations in and near her home. In hysterics, she spouted wicked conspiracy theories regarding the disaster and involuntary sedation was required. Patient to be released temporarily to prepare herself for an indefinite inpatient stay.

Margaret signed herself out that day and the ambulance driver watched her walk to her front door. But later that night, mom made one final trek out to Forget Me Knot rock. Barefoot, wrapped only in the same thin cotton nightgown as before, she'd polished off her last bottle of Canadian Club before descending the stairs to the beach. But there was no low tide this time. The next day, Thanksgiving morning, Leslie's father discovered Mrs. Margaret Preston at the base of Forget-Me-Knot, facedown and half-buried in silt.

And where was I during all this? In Portland, winding down my first semester at college and grateful as hell to be far away. Bus ticket in hand, I was reluctantly packing for my holiday trip home when my RA knocked on my door. "Boyd, you have a call."

Cancel the "indefinite inpatient stay" order for Mrs. Boyd at Evergreen Sanitarium. I had no more heart to break

My hands shook as I reread that final entry in her medical records: *reports seeing and interacting with a member of the* USS *Stryker crew.* So, I wasn't the only one. Hayes had pulled the same stunt (or something like it) on my mother, too, stealing her last remaining crumbs of happiness and sanity. He might as well have walked her straight into the waves himself.

Who knows? Maybe he did.

A word of advice: if you're planning on going crazy, don't do it in the cafeteria of a mental institution. I snatched up my mother's records and knocked over my chair in a frenzied rush toward the nearest EXIT sign. My jog down the sterile hallway escalated into a full sprint, clutching her doctors' notes to my chest, all that remained of my betrayed, unsalvageable mother. Breathless, I barreled into an employee, sending her sprawling to the floor. The others scattered, eyes wide and pressed against the walls, awaiting a code-red alarm that a patient had gone off the rails.

Off the rails? Hell yes. But not even the strongest drugs or the nuttiest shrinks on the hospital's staff could fix me. I was in a different kind of storm. I knew how Margaret felt.

But maybe, just maybe, there was still a place where I could center myself, where I could think this through.

C'mon, Jenny. Focus. Think.

I glanced at today's tide tables. Yep, I had a couple hours before high tide.

Let's go, time's a'wastin'!

Forget Me Knot

At first, I didn't think it was Blanche. Dozens of gulls, an indistinguishable, shifting mass, had claimed Forget Me Knot rock as their territory. But no. Wait... it *was* her! Let's see: missing half of her right foot, a snow-white neck and face framed by jet-black wings... and, of course, that unmistakable attitude. *This is my rock. What the hell are YOU doing here?*

I know, I know. Ridiculous, right? Who even knows if Blanche is female? And do seagulls really have personalities? But then again... what did my mother's file say again? *Seeing things that aren't there.* Brilliant. Evergreen Sanitarium, here I come.

Forget Me Knot Rock was Boyd's Cove's only legit tourist attraction. Now, we're not a college town, but we *do* know how to spell. To honor the local fishermen, a marketing genius at the Chamber added a "K" to the name back in '70, and it stuck. Gotta admit, I liked it. It's the perfect tourist tell—like the people who visit New York City and butcher Houston Street as if they're in Texas.

Sea to summit, the basalt monolith rose forty feet tall, a miniature Half Dome rising from the surf. In summer, bored teenagers claimed it, carving initials, cryptic graffiti, and Cupid arrows into its weathered face. The inlet that cradled Knot Rock was shallow—so shallow that at low tide, a muddy peninsula surfaced, tethering it to the beach. An aluminum sign, stamped with a glow-in-the-dark skull and crossbones, marked the spit's entrance, warning visitors to check the tide tables.

But its real message was timeless and more profound: the sea ain't your friend. Ignore her fickleness and indifference at your own peril.

The Knot wasn't just for teenagers and tourists. Just a mile from my cottage (with a fine view from my childhood bedroom), it used to be a regular Boyd family destination. On Saturday afternoons, my father would snatch a stone from the beach and show off his outfielder's arm by flinging it toward the Knot. He always aimed for the top of the escarpment, the long, flat slope facing the shore. A devoted Yankees fan, he was forever Joe DiMaggio, gunning down a Cardinal or Giant at the plate who dared tag up on a fly ball to center. I'd play umpire, call the runner safe, which set off his playful theatrics.

What! Are you blind? Your glass eye fog up on that one?

Got a challenge for you: ask an older person how long ago it was they did something.

Hey, Pops, how long ago did you make that cross-country drive?

Or... *Aunt Julia, how many years since you went to Disneyland with the grandkids?*

"Oh, five, maybe seven years ago, dear."

"No, try fifteen, Auntie."

With age, time becomes fluid. We squeeze decades into years, years into yesterday. Our estimates round up, always toward the present, never the past.

But there are exceptions to this cliché. For example, I'm bulletproof, bet-the-house sure on the timing of my last trek to Forget-Me-Knot Rock: November 23, 1953.

The day after my mother was found.

Wading out to the outcropping, I gingerly picked my way through, around, and over the slippery rocks until I reached the tide pool where she'd been discovered. Even for a kid, the spot wasn't hard to find that day. Hours earlier, the beach had been trampled by forensics teams, police, and looky-loos. Cigarette butts littered the scene. Gulls sniffed the air. Judging by the picnic trash and fading footprints, it was clear the whole town had satisfied its curiosity.

To an eight-year-old, this was the real horror. In my prepubescent mind, I—and I alone—had missed the signs of her demise, signs visible to everyone but me. Not only had Boyd's Cove's gossipy predictions about my "unstable" mother come true, but the town couldn't resist hovering like black-winged vultures, eager to see for themselves.

So that's why. You didn't ask, but there you have it. For forty years, I hadn't set foot on this rock. Until today.

I climbed steadily toward the peak. Not a scramble like the last time I was here, a race-to-the-top dash by a teen in a sundress. Instead, it was a slow, cautious climb built on experience, with three points of contact at all times. At the summit, I nestled into a nook on the leeward side, shielded from the wind.

A perfect place to contemplate a lifetime of misplaced grief and gratitude.

What was I left with? Emotional bets placed on all the wrong horses. Parlays gone empty, every wager lost. My father's legacy—the mental Alamo I'd barricaded behind whenever my life went south—was a lie. My mother, a true victim in both life and death, had fared no better. Revolted by her weakness and addiction, I had condemned her long ago.

And let's not forget good ol' Medford Jerry. In the shadow of my parental ghosts, I'd exiled an innocent husband, clueless that he was competing for my affection against a double-crossing traitor.

What about Boyd's Cove itself? Magnanimously claiming credit for supporting me while letting the Navy pay off its bribes? That's some serious brass balls.

And now, in the irony of all ironies, in just forty-eight hours, Boyd's Cove would bestow its highest honor on its namesake son. Our own little patriotic Woodstock was about to kick off. Navy brass, news media from *Sixty Minutes* to KGW cub reporters, and descendants of the *Stryker* crew were boarding flights as we spoke. Nothing was left to chance for the grand occasion. We'd even declared a school holiday to guarantee packed sidewalks for the noon parade. Fourth of July bunting was hauled out of storage, draping the Fog Cutter and her neighbors in the glory of Old Glory. Rexall's Drug posted a sign apologizing for running out of camera batteries and umbrellas. The fuse was lit, the orchestra primed, and the ball was ready to drop.

The crumpled paper in my raincoat pocket spelled out the next two days in exhausting detail. Day One started with parade kickoff remarks. As Grand Marshal, I'd wave elegantly from the backseat of Cal Tipton's Packard One Twenty touring sedan. Once the street cleared, fire the cap gun to start the 10K race to the veterans' cemetery and back. At 4 p.m., drive up to the new Preston C. Boyd Coast Guard base for the ribbon-cutting ceremony before wrapping up with local media interviews.

Tired yet? Buckle up. Day Two was the main event.

Hair and makeup at 9 a.m. with CBS, followed by an interview with Harry Reasoner. With the *Stryker* monument in Boyd Park as the backdrop, a boyish producer would urge me to give the *60 Minutes* audience an "unvarnished account" of what it "felt like as an eight-year-old to lose your father so close to home." After the tears, Harry would compose himself and praise me for my "unwavering courage" and "lifetime of service." Shoot a little B-roll of Forget Me Knot, snap some publicity shots, and call it a wrap: a fifteen-minute feel-good story for America after a Sunday afternoon of midseason football.

"Well, what would you do, Blanche?"

The other gulls broke away, drawn to a fishing boat and its half-full nets just outside The Cove. But not this one. Blanche (if it was her) kept me company as I huddled against the wind. We all know that signs and omens are a crock: just coincidences disguised as meaning. But then again, so are uniformed spirits invading my kitchen. I settled the argument with myself once and for all. This gull *was* Blanche from The Cutter, and she'd help me figure this out.

And in a way she did.

The gulls of Boyd's Cove—or Bodega Bay, Huntington Beach, Eureka, take your pick—wheel overhead without a second glance. They're all the same, aren't they? A blur of wings, a squawking flock. Never one bird, no Jonathan Livingston, never a singular entity.

If there's a better metaphor for my life, I haven't found it. Always visible, but never seen. Not even by myself.

But it's all clear now.

Thank you, Margaret.

For holding on as long as you did. For sacrificing your sanity to give me a fighting chance to retreat safely to the rear.

You saw past the noise, past the flock, into the one unique bird that was me. A bird who could do more than watch from the sidelines.

A bird who could act.

I'd agonized over difficult, no-win decisions in my life. But tomorrow? Tomorrow was no longer one of them. Man your battle stations. Time to refloat the *Stryker* and salvage what remained of the truth.

Mr. Reasoner and his peach fuzz producer would never forget their sit-down with the mayor of Boyd Cove.

Office of the Historian

"**G**et on up here Reef!"

Back home from my Forget Me Knot vision quest, I poured myself a cocoa and cleared a spot on the couch for my pug to joyously join me. Only my cat-like reflexes kept my fresh cup of Swiss Miss from total disaster.

Almost.

My penguin-on-land clumsiness is no myth. Hot chocolate sloshed over the brim, cascading into a miniature chocolate waterfall that joined the pug's technicolor gallery of stains already tattooed into the couch. Not for the first time, I cursed my younger, thriftier self for shrugging off the salesman's cheery advice: "It's just a couple bucks more for the Stain Guard!"

Next time, I'm Stain-Guarding the whole damn house. Maybe the pug, too.

Boundaries between Reef and me didn't exist, especially during his favorite TV shows. He'd sprawl on the couch, unfazed by my awkward little game of couch Twister to carve out some space. Tonight, Reef was extra pumped—and why not? It was Tuesday, ABC's top-rated, big-money lineup.

Onscreen, the needle dropped and Bill Haley's "Rock Around the Clock" filled the room. Perfect. A mindless *Happy Days* episode to ease me into the evening, with *Laverne & Shirley* waiting to tuck me in. Just what the doctor ordered.

I felt better—better than I had in a week. Maybe better than before this all began. With a deep sigh, I scratched Reef's head, stretched out on the couch, and propped my feet up on the ottoman. The first sip of hot chocolate was perfect: warm and sweet, with the marshmallows melted just right.

If you haven't picked up on it by now, I'm not exactly Miss Organized. You don't want me planning your wedding. My motto's always been: *Why do today what I can put off until tomorrow?* All week long, I'd dreaded tonight, picturing a late-night slog of drafting and rehearsing speeches for the *Stryker* ceremonies. But with the truth finally out, I could kiss that homework goodbye. Bye-bye, speeches. Hello, peace of mind.

Why? Because I now knew *exactly* what I was going to say. Those scribbled speech drafts? Ashes in the fire. Did I thank all the right people or wear the most flattering outfit? Moot, meaningless questions. After I revealed the truth to Harry and the rest of America, no one would be gossiping about my hair color or counting my stammers. This wouldn't be small talk fodder—it would be a Kennedy moment. A real life *where-were-you-when* shock brought to you by little ol' Boyd's Cove.

Have other plans? Cancel 'em. You're not gonna want to miss this must-see TV.

Fonzie had just jump-started Al's skipping jukebox with his magic elbow when the doorbell chimed. Reef barked like the UPS guy had declared war. I groaned, shuffled into my robe, and yanked the terry-cloth belt tight. The bell went off again—ding-dong, ding-dong. Did they not think I was home? I was always home.

"I'm coming, I'm coming!"

I peered through the front drapes before opening the door. A sleek, black Fleetwood Cadillac idled in the driveway, its headlights cutting through the evening drizzle. The engine purred softly, a hum out of place among Boyd's Cove's pickup trucks and station wagons.

The passenger-side door opened, and a man stepped out, silhouetted by the greenish glow of the dashboard lights. He adjusted his coat against the mist, his shoes splashing through driveway puddles as he made his way to the porch. A second figure joined him, hunched against the wind.

A Cadillac? In Boyd's Cove? My stomach tightened. What the hell was this all about?

I flipped on the porch light and cracked the front door. Two middle-aged men stood there, oblivious to the rain. The naval officer wore a fitted blue blazer with buff lapels. Gold epaulets adorned the forearms of both sleeves, and his left breast was splashed with medals—so much tin I doubted even he could tell me what each one was for.

He was tall, so tall he had to duck to avoid the porch overhang. Removing his cover, he tucked it under his left arm, giving me my first good look at him. His weathered face spoke of a life spent outdoors, yet he'd managed to preserve a pair of kind eyes, which squinted at me through the doorway.

"Ms. Boyd, I presume." The quiet, confident voice matched the officer's executive presence.

My heart racing, I could only stare. So much for my couch night with Reef.

"I am Admiral James Goodman, commander of the US Pacific Fleet. I hope you'll call me Jim."

He turned to the man standing beside him.

"And this is Dr. Miles Albright, Secretary of the Office of the Historian, a division of the U.S. State Department."

The admiral's companion was half his height and twice as nervous. His brown corduroy jacket, elbow patches and all, might have fit ten years ago but now strained across his frame. Out of breath, he gave a slight bow as he introduced himself, his soaked glasses perilously close to sliding off his nose. His beard was a bushy, Jerry Garcia-style thicket streaked with gray

It was the first thought that came to mind. "I've never heard of the Office of the Historian."

Mr. Hollywood Navy man, a doppelganger mix of Harrison Ford and Robert Mitchum, chuckled.

"Very understandable, Ms. Boyd. Neither had I until very, very recently. May we come in?"

Wordlessly, I turned toward the kitchen. My cottage had been a guest-free zone for years. I refused the commander's chivalrous offer of help and dragged an extra chair from my bedroom so the three of us could sit at the kitchen table. The admiral took his place with his back to the drywall—still unpainted—where Seaman Hayes had carved out his nocturnal excavation a few nights ago. Once the tea kettle was on, I took a seat across from my visitors. How surreal was this?

After some pleasantries about the cottage (and Reef), Admiral Goodman got to the point.

"Ms. Boyd, you've been kind enough to receive us unannounced on a rainy night. And, on the night before what I'm sure will be a very busy day for you tomorrow. You deserve to know the purpose of our visit and so you shall. Mr. Albright?"

The bureaucrat took a final sip of his tea and cleared his throat a little too loudly. He fished out a binder from a leather satchel he'd been clutching like a purse and placed it on the table. A red-and-white banner, stenciled across the cover, stared back at me.

Top Secret - Level 5 eyes only

After one final, unnecessary cough, he was ready. "Ms. Boyd—may I call you Jenny?" I nodded, my eyes fixed on the binder. "You mentioned you've never heard of the Office of the Historian. A brief background, if I may."

"I'm the Secretary in charge of this office. We're responsible for keeping a comprehensive historical record of the dealings of the United States with foreign countries. Our office was created back in 1919, just after World War I, and is tasked with the preservation of America's foreign policy record. We also make recommendations to the Foreign Service based on past successes and failures."

He paused, hesitantly reaching for another sip of tea, but he'd already drained his cup. Assuming we wouldn't notice, he carried on.

"Now, before your eyes glaze over, let's get to why this matters to you. There's a top-secret department within the Office that handles only the most highly classified material. Yesterday, I received an urgent call from Admiral Goodman.

He relayed a conversation he'd had with a Ms. Leslie Watson regarding your father's role in the sinking of the USS *Stryker*."

I didn't just feel the blood leaving my head—I heard it.

Batten down the hatches.

My hands clenched the edges of the chair to fend off what was coming next. A breath. Then another.

No use. The room tilted. Here it comes...

A tornado of dizziness touched down in my skull, spinning and swirling. It wasn't just the room. It was my thoughts. My focus. My ability to think at all.

My head fell into my hands. I gasped as the world pulsed around me, a seismic quake tearing through my senses.

At this point, the Admiral earned another medal to add to his victory garden. He grasped my right hand and scooted his chair closer, bridging the distance between us.

"It's OK, Jenny. Breathe. Just breathe. It's going to be alright."

Was it? Was it really?

"In and out, in and out. There we go."

And there it went. His distraction calmed the earthquake, and I slowly opened my eyes. The Admiral—Jim?—pressed a glass of water into my trembling hands and made sure I drank the whole thing. The tempest settled back into the neuronal caves of my brain, on standby to flare during my next self-generated freak-out.

"I'm OK, I'm OK," I insisted as the aftershocks subsided. "A cup of water, please."

I straightened myself up to hear the rest of this. But first...

"Let me get this straight: Sheriff Leslie Watson called the Navy to rat me out, saying she'd finally told me the truth?"

Reasonably sure at this point that I wasn't going to end up on the floor, Admiral Jim released my hand. I do love one thing about military people: they're direct. No sugarcoating. No sandwiching bad news with good. They just answer the question.

"That's correct, ma'am. She did. The Navy has had a long-standing agreement with Ms. Watson: if certain facts became known to you at any point, she was to contact us immediately."

Shocked, I put my hand over my mouth. Maybe I was going to throw up after all. The Admiral took advantage of this lapse in my defenses to seize the initiative.

"Jenny, that's HOW we got here. If you give us a chance, we'll tell you WHY. Miles?"

Albright cleared his throat yet again and took the reins.

"Sure. First, let's make sure you understand the basics. You're under the impression that your father's intentions that night were to turn over his sub to the Japanese, correct?"

I nodded. The Admiral was holding my hand again. Or had I reached for it?

"So, this is where it gets byzantine. Before I begin, I must inform you that, even to this day, everything I'm about to tell you remains highly classified. Now, I—we—realize that once we relay this information, we have no control over what you do with it. You haven't signed any waiver, and we have no legal power to prevent you from talking to others as you see fit." He glanced over at the Admiral for assurance. "However, Admiral Goodman and I are confident that once you have the full story, you'll understand why it had to happen this way."

The Admiral turned towards me.

"But it's more than that. Jenny, after all these years, you deserve to know the real truth about your father and what happened that night."

I leaned back in my chair and folded my arms.

"I can't—and I won't—make any promises. Everything's been a lie up to this point and, hey, maybe this is too."

Mildly alarmed, my visitors looked at each other. For a moment, I thought they were going to get up and disappear into the night. But they'd come this far. Then the historian did what historians do.

Storytime.

"Ms. Boyd—Jenny—back in the late '20s, before you were born, before your father even met your mother, he served as a Foreign Service Officer in Yokohama, Japan. His official title was naval attaché, but he actually worked for Naval Intelligence. During this time, the Japanese nationalist movement was gaining strength. His job was to recruit local civilians who were unsympathetic to right-wing politics so we could better understand what was going on internally within the Japanese government."

"So you're saying my father was a spy?"

Albright and Goodman exchanged glances again.

"That's exactly what I'm saying."

Albright continued. "Lieutenant Boyd—he was promoted to Captain later, in 1936—gained the confidence of a Ms. Miyuki Yamacho, a civil servant in the National Socialist Japanese Workers Party. Yamacho-san had been educated in the United States and spoke perfect English."

Stop the tape. I know, the smart thing to do here would have been to pretend. Pretend I didn't know this already. Nod silently, string them along. Squeeze every ounce of information from them while revealing nothing myself.

But I was too tired to play cloak-and-dagger games. Let's skip all this, go directly to "Pass Go" and collect our $200.

"Yes, yes, I know all this. They were lovers."

I'd flipped the script. Or, in Navy terms, "crossed the T." It was their turn to be shocked. The Admiral broke in. No way this skirmish was going to spin out of control on his watch.

"Yes, Jenny. Not sure how you knew that, but yes, they were. Dr. Albright, please continue."

The historian obeyed. "So, you might ask, why would the Navy be interested in a low-level bureaucrat with limited access to sensitive information? Well, Ms. Yamacho was the only daughter of Admiral Takatsugu Yamacho, commander of the *Kido Butai*, the largest combined carrier battle group in the Imperial Japanese Navy."

Albright pressed on. "Due to your father's intel, we learned that Admiral Yamacho was a widower and Miyuki his only child. Having spent time in the States, the Admiral recognized the limitless resources America had to prosecute the war and was opposed to the Pearl Harbor attack. But, of course, his concerns were dismissed by Tojo and the rest of the War Ministry."

Albright opened a folder, removed a document, and placed it in front of me on the kitchen table.

"And thanks to your father and the courage of Ms. Yamacho, the Navy was aware all along of his severe misgivings. Which led to a once-in-a-wartime opportunity."

The cable read:

July 21, 1942: Dear Preston - Father can no longer participate in this madness. He seeks to end this terrible war as soon as humanly possible. Defection is the only option. By sharing his knowledge of the Imperial Navy's strategy he could save thousands of lives. The cause is lost. Honor demands this course.

Always Yours,

Miyuki

I reread the yellowed telegram and then read it again. Good old Seaman Hayes knew about my father's letters, but the poor bastard must have known nothing of these cables. I rubbed my eyes as an even bigger realization hit me.

Everyone (minus Quinn!) had noble intentions every step of the way. And, despite this, it still all crashed and burned. This wasn't your typical, that-really-sucks tragedy. This was Montague and Capulet level—a Romeo and Juliet horror show that destroyed sailors, families, and maybe even blew a chance to end mankind's bloodiest war ahead of schedule.

A question for the archivist. I accepted a tissue from Admiral Jim and fired away.

"So, did my mother."

Albright had anticipated my query.

"From what we can tell, Miyuki knew that after your father left Japan, he married and had a child—you." He looked over at the Navy officer. "But it's unclear—in fact, unlikely—that your mother knew anything at all about the existence of Miyuki Yamacho."

I sat back, stunned. The impossible was starting to make sense. "But things obviously didn't go as planned."

It was the Admiral's turn.

"No, they didn't, to say the least. Captain Boyd was scheduled to accept the defection of Admiral Yamacho during a scheduled rendezvous with the *Hibiki*, a destroyer-class vessel, on November 15, 1942." He paused. "And you spoke to Liam Quinn, so I think you know the rest. An out-of-context remark overheard by Seaman Hayes led to a well-intentioned—but ultimately disastrous—mutiny."

I stood up from the table and turned my back to them. Goodman and Albright gave me a moment to process. When I turned around, the questions poured out.

"Why couldn't the Navy just tell the truth at the time?"

"That would have jeopardized the lives of both the Admiral and his daughter, as well as the possibility of any future engagement with them."

"What ended up happening to Miyuki's father, the Japanese Admiral?"

"The Imperial Navy recognized his lack of enthusiasm for the war and exiled him to a desk in Singapore. Killed in an air raid in 1944."

"Why, after all these years, is the cover-up still in place?"

"There was one and only one condition from Miyuki Yamacho in exchange for her cooperation. While she's still alive, no one can ever know the role she and her father played in trying to end the war sooner. In her opinion, the disgrace of collaborating with the enemy would ruin her life. She lives in Kyushu now and has a family of her own."

My questions answered, I pushed my chair in and they took the cue. Time to go. Rather than wait for them to ask, I took the helm.

"So what do you expect me to do? The whole world is here for the *Stryker*. Just ignore all this and go along with the lies?"

The Admiral stood up slowly and retrieved his cover from the chair he'd set it on. He turned it over and placed it under his left arm.

"Ma'am, as I said in the very beginning, what you do with this knowledge is solely up to you."

He led the way to the front door as Albright grabbed his satchel. I closed the door behind them as he started up the Cadillac. Its taillights blinked once before disappearing down the driveway, taking away both the visitors and my peace of mind.

Felon

Here's some trivia for your next cocktail party.

Dante described the nine rings of Hell. But did you know there was originally a tenth? Without the poet's permission, his editor slashed the final chapter from *The Divine Comedy* ("the pacing felt a little slow"), a sin that surely landed the hack in his own toasty room-with-a-view in Hades.

Fortunately, this tenth ring survived the Medici, Prohibition, and disco, and lives on today as a sadistic high school assignment. Introverts will recognize this task for what it is—a teenage torture on par with Sadie Hawkins dances ("Girls don't wait—ask a boy now before they're all taken!") and algebra word problems.

Ready for the big reveal? Drumroll, please...

Memorize and recite a famous historical passage in front of your fellow students.

I wasn't the only kid freaked out by this exercise. Cue up the groans when Mrs. Carlson passed out the recitation schedule. Although the veteran educator passionately taught us the wonders of Western democracy, the actual practice of it in her classroom was *verboten*. We weren't voting or coming to consensus on any decisions in Room 3A. At the faintest whiff of dissent, she'd mount a steel-booted assault to crush any and all resistance.

Don't you dare question my academic methods! Rote memorization and the ability to recite in front of your classmates is a critical skill you'll need in life! Besides, it's just the Gettysburg Address. Only 272 words. No big deal. Practice and you'll do fine.

So I did. A lot. But my tearful days of stammering bedroom mirror rehearsals were followed by nightly dreams of bitchy Stacy Thompson and her mascara groupies, convulsed in whispered, cool-girl laughter. I didn't successfully make my way through a practice speech once—not a single time. Finally, the fateful day arrived.

"All right, class, settle down. Jenny Boyd, your turn. Come to the front of the room. No dilly-dallying, let's go."

My performance that day is still a popular topic at class reunions. A stark, SAT-like terror washed over me on my way to the front of the classroom. Breaths came in ragged, shallow gasps. My feet might have touched the floor. They also might not have. I stared past the eager honor roll students in the front row, past the gum-chewing juvies in the back, and focused on a casket-sized, 48-star American flag draped across the chalkboard.

Big mistake.

When fear takes over, muscle memory kicks in. Last semester, we recited the Preamble to the Constitution. With that big ol' flag just a-starin' at me, well... you can guess what happened next.

"We the people, in order to form..."

Stacy and her gang of Stacies were merciless. No way could this hysterical f-up be forgotten or forgiven. For the rest of the school year, I heard it echoing in the hallways: "We the people, fourscore and seven years ago..."

The "D" from Mrs. Carlson also didn't help (I ended up delivering Lincoln's Address to her after school).

But here's the weird part: although I hate to admit it, the rote memorization camp has a point. When you burn stuff—passages, baseball statistics, hatred of Stacy Thompson—into a still-developing brain, it sticks. Need proof? Just look in the last pew of this morning's 8 a.m. Mass at St. Andrew's by the Sea.

I'd snuck in the back after the incense-infused entrance procession. There hadn't been church in my life since my twenties. I'd flippantly tell proselytizers at The Barnacle that I didn't abandon organized religion; it abandoned me. Truth is, I'm the one who called the dump truck. Yet, twenty years later, here I am, chanting not only the greatest hits (Our Father, Hail Mary), but keeping my missal closed for the longer B-side tunes as well (even made it all the way through the Apostles' Creed). Early memories are like tenants in rent-controlled apartments: unevictable and they stick around forever.

Father Fitzgerald's house of worship was more than half full; a rarity outside of Easter, Christmas, and the biannual high school DWI funeral. Sneezing and coughing, a couple of press hounds hung back near the confessional booth. A dozen or so out-of-towners bowed their heads, mostly widows and children of long-dead *Stryker* men.

Which reminded me.

At 10 a.m., I was scheduled to meet with these relatives at The Barnacle (before the noon parade). Of course, I'd completely forgotten about it.

Jesus. What was I supposed to say to them?

I'd been humming along with the service, half-enjoying myself. I didn't come for the sermon, which was a good thing. When Father Mike started pounding the pulpit on the wickedness of birth control, I mentally crossed off any future plans to congregate at St. Andrews by the Sea. Well... maybe Easter and Christmas.

The reason I'd actually come sat in the front row (like she always did), kneeling and signing the cross in sync with the other believers. Sheriff Leslie, already in uniform, was physically—and now morally—ready to protect and serve us on Preston Boyd Day. At our weekly Cutter breakfast catch-ups, I'd pretend to be impressed if she'd dry-cleaned her jacket or indulged in her once-a-year manicure. But today was no joke. Ready for inspection, she looked Academy-fresh with her polished brass and West Point-straight gig line. Thank god at least one of us looked the part. I know people were tired of seeing me in my Kmart Jaclyn Smith blazer and black Wrangler jeans.

Too bad.

During communion, I slipped out to wait by Leslie's just-washed Crown Victoria, courtesy of the Boyd Cove High School girls' softball team, who'd been shaking us down for the past six months to pay for a Disneyland tournament. She spotted me while shaking hands with Father Mike (even though I knew she thought his sermon was trash) and headed over, all business.

Arms crossed, hat dipped over one eye, she'd skipped her morning dose of Skoal. It was The Law stood before me, not Leslie.

She took the first swing.

"Jenny Boyd in the house of the Lord? Leavin' nothing to chance on the big day now, are we?"

That used to be true.

For so long, I'd cared deeply about today. After two years of planning, tracking down *Stryker* relatives all over the country and a case of Pepto-Bismol, PB Day was finally here. More than my wedding, more than my graduations, more than my first election, these forty-eight hours would define my legacy. Was I up to it? As a mayor, as a daughter, as a don't-call-me-crazy-anymore legit adult?

But, as the song says, that was yesterday. Fact is, I no longer cared. For the first time in a long while—maybe ever—I knew where I stood. Everyone else? That was their problem.

"Guess it's not just me. You're looking mighty spiffy, Sheriff. Maybe the TV people should interview you instead."

A cautious laugh. "With my potty mouth? Bleepin' this, bleepin' that? Nah, I'll leave the talkin' to the professionals."

My mouth went through the motions of a smile, but Leslie caught the ice in my eyes.

"Speaking of professionals," I said, "two visitors stopped by last night. One in a uniform almost as sharp as yours."

To her credit, she held my gaze and let out a long, slow whistle. "Well, that was quick. If the swabbies had been this fast on the draw back in '41, December 7th would've just been another tropical Hawaiian Sunday morning."

"You told'em."

"Damn right I did."

"After you finally came clean to me in The Cutter yesterday—held my hands in OUR childhood booth—you weren't done. Nope. Played me again. No heads-up. No, 'Hey Jenny, by the way, I'm going to let the goddamn government in on our little conversation.' My best friend... a double agent."

Fists balled, I waited for a counterpunch. But she was unfazed. My words washed over her, dissipating into the morning air. Fresh from Mass, St. Leslie turned the other cheek. Sorry, officer, but that Sermon on the Mount stuff wasn't going to work for me. Not today.

Instead, I committed my first-ever felony that morning, right there in the St. Andrews parking lot. I launched myself like a linebacker into the Boyd's Cove Sheriff, pinning her against the Victoria. She let out a stunned "oof" as her Smokey the Bear hat tumbled across the roof and landed in the gravel. Chin-to-chin, I grabbed her cop lapels and shook her so hard her "Watson" name tag came unclipped, joining her hat in the dirt.

I can't remember exactly what I said during the beatdown, other than a few "bastards" and "I actually thought we were friends." With no resistance from my opponent, my fury fizzled out like a dud firecracker. My debut assault and battery ended not in triumph, but in a pitiful, tear-streaked whimper.

Spent, I collapsed to the ground, my back pressed against the Ford's front bumper. Like an umpire after a catcher gets smashed with a foul tip, Leslie gave me a moment. She took her sweet time retrieving her hat, patting around for the missing name tag clip. Finally, she came around to the front, grabbed my sobbing self by the shoulders, and guided me into the car.

The front seat, by the way—not the back.

After turning off the hyperactive scanner, Leslie stared ahead through the just-Windexed windshield. Humming, she pulled down the visor to check her reflection in the cop car's vanity mirror. In a week already packed with shocking surprises, here came another. From her Batman-inspired utility belt, Sheriff Watson produced a lipstick tube. Not the light pink Revlon or boring Maybelline gloss. That would've been disconcerting enough. No, this was a forty-eight-year-old woman I hadn't seen wear makeup since senior prom, now wielding an Orange Crush-flavored Bonnie Bell Lip Smacker to doll herself up.

Meanwhile, the instigator of the brawl lay slumped in defeat in the passenger seat. There was no hand-holding or coffee talk this time. As the early bird senior citizens limped toward the church for the 9:30 a.m. mass, Leslie broke the silence with a sigh. Her first words, though, weren't for me.

"Daddy, you were right. It wasn't easy."

Then, she turned her attention to the living.

"You know Jenny, we're friends. Good friends. Best friends. Got time for a story on Preston Boyd Day?"

Leslie's tone hardened with the memory.

"There was one other chick at the Academy with me back in '58. One from a class of fifty. Emily Porter. We slogged through all the basic training nonsense together. The drill instructors didn't mess with me too much. Everybody knew who my father was, and that bought me a wide berth. But Emily? She got the full treatment. Hazing stuff that would never fly today."

Her pace quickened as those days flooded back.

"But we'd both made it. Only a week till graduation. And we got one night of leave. It was Cinderella rules—be back in the barracks by midnight. And guess who drew the short straw? Yours truly. I was the cadet on guard that night, pen in hand, responsible for signing every last one of 'em in and out.

"Midnight comes. No Emily. One o'clock, two o'clock—nada. Finally, it's 0500. Thirty minutes before reveille. She stumbles into the guard shack, hair a mess, begging me to sign her in—*before* midnight."

She paused and licked her glossed lips so hard they were gonna need another coat.

"But there's a problem. The police cadet honor code: '*A cadet will not lie, cheat, steal, or tolerate those who do.*' I'm a twenty two-year-old bushy-tailed rookie, and now I have to decide: where do my loyalties lie? Am I a low-life snitch? Or do ideals—duty, honor—fancy words that don't go to your wedding or help you over the obstacle course wall—trump friendship?"

Heavy indeed. She summed up her thinking.

"So I made my choice. Friendship has limits. Personal honor does not. I gave my word to my father and the Navy all those years ago. Yesterday, they cashed the check. Once I made the promise, the money was theirs, not mine. So was the choice difficult? Yes. But was it simple? Also yes."

As she pulled out of the parking lot, St. Andrew's bell tolled, a mournful witness to a sisters-like bond forever changed. I'd never understood her churchgoing ways. It always seemed hypocritical, as if her foul-mouthed insouciance could be erased by an hour of mumbling devotions each Sunday.

But, as with so much in my own life, I'd missed the clue sitting right in front of me. In her religion, her patriotism, and her life, Leslie was living for a higher power. And had been all along.

There's that pattern again. Last one to see the ship taking on water. And the lifeboats? Nearly gone.

The Leftovers

I went to the church seeking revenge.

I went to the bar seeking redemption.

I was half an hour late, but I wasn't the only one. The gloomy marine layer that KOBI-TV promised would burn off in time for the parade still hung low, sour and gray. Meanwhile, the overzealous Knights of Columbus volunteers wielding traffic cones like they owned the street weren't helping my tardiness. Two hours early for their shift, the geezers had already cordoned off Main Street for the noon parade. And trust me—being Mayor didn't earn me any special privileges.

Forced to ditch my Bronco two blocks away, I clip-clopped down the sidewalk in my never-worn (and almost-not-found) heels to The Barnacle. On the debit side of the ledger, I'd managed to clean up the tear streaks and in-car screaming. But the puffiness in my cheeks lingered as if I'd been on a steroid binge.

Oh well. Lucky for me, half the lights were broken or burnt out anyway. And I was late. Maybe that was a blessing. Everyone was probably on their second Bloody Mary by now.

No such luck. Cokes and iced teas only for this crowd. Maybe ten older women, a few middle-aged men. I recognized a couple of them from church. Pilgrims from across the country, they'd spent the night at the Brookings Best Western or maybe a Motel 6 down in Crescent City. Their luggage tags gave 'em away: LAX, DFW, even as far east as PHI. Overtired from their flight connections and underwhelmed by The Barnacle's Long John Silver decor, the *Stryker* parents and children waited expectantly.

Waited for me.

I whispered to Cody, the unlucky bartender stuck with this special morning shift, to leave the vodka out of my usual. Cranberry juice in hand, I slid into the empty seat at the head of the pushed-together plastic tables.

The side chatter trickled down to a murmur, then nothing. All eyes were on me.

But as I leaned forward to introduce myself, the darndest thing happened.

Sparked by a prematurely graying lady from SFO in the back, they began clapping. People I'd never met. At first, it was polite; a smattering of golf claps, nothing more. But then it swelled, escalating into a full-throated ovation. Cheers with a couple of "Bravo!"s, tossed in for good measure, as if I'd just wrapped a curtain call instead of showing up late with puffy eyes and cranberry juice.

Applause for nothing. For services never rendered.

I hadn't heard a crowd like that since I was fifteen, standing stiff before the Boyd Cove faithful as they handed me my college money.

Maybe life is a circle after all.

The puffiness in my cheeks returned. My grateful reaction (yes, I cried again, at least the third time this morning) only encouraged the applause to loiter, stretching embarrassingly long. Finally, an annoyed Cody ended the nonsense with a gunshot-loud crack of a wet towel from behind the bar, snapping us all back to reality.

"Thank you for that, Cody. Our eardrums thank you as well." I didn't mention this was an old Barnacle trick to scare off the daytime mice. Bolder than their nocturnal cousins, these feisty critters were fearless as they scavenged the sticky floor for peanut shells and beer nuts. Temporarily cowed, they watched from the shadows. The floor was mine.

"Thank you, thank you all so much. As most of you probably know, I'm Jenny Boyd, mayor of Boyd's Cove, and daughter of Captain Preston Boyd. Apologies for being late, but we still have about an hour before the parade starts. I thought we could go around the table, introduce ourselves, and share a few words about the loved one you lost on the *Stryker*."

Just as Flo from Michigan was about to tell us about her older brother Al, I couldn't help myself and veered off-script. "By the way, any relatives of Seaman Hayes here this morning?"

Silence. Sigh. Just as well. Especially since I was only drinking cranberry juice.

Around the horn they went. Jake Sullivan's brother won the Dallas-Fort Worth pancake-eating contest. Robert "Bob" Henderson was a lights-out shortstop, but the Giants passed on him because he couldn't hit a curveball. And that rascal, sixteen-year-old Travis Bennett, used a fake mustache to fool the Des Moines Navy recruiter, determined to keep his fixed appointment with death just five months later.

This crew of left-behinders had traveled a long way, and no doubt, had many stories to tell. So, I was surprised by how brief their monologues were. Halfway through, it hit me.

They were here for me. My story. That's why they clapped. After all, I had been here, on the scene, closest to the action. They each had their own memories of the dreaded "we-regret-to-inform-you" telegram and the casualty officer's knock on the door. But on that ordinary, world-changing, full moon evening, I had been physically closest to their loved ones.

Tell us everything, their eyes demanded. Leave nothing out.

I didn't intend to. Besides, the parade couldn't start without me. Oh well. The K of C boys in their goofy hats would have yet another reason to think I'm a ditz.

So, like Genesis and most relationships, I started at the beginning. The very beginning. I kicked things off with a carousel of snapshots from my eight years with Father, drawing chuckles over his Creature from the Black Lagoon prank and tears over our last day together at Forget Me Knot Rock.

And then, Act 2, a minute-by-minute account of that fateful day. The Indian summer weather, the drawn blackout curtains. How I went to sleep whole, and woke up a candle blown out mid-flame.

On to the epilogue, into the decades of numbness. Past Margaret's suicide, with a nod to my stints at Evergreen. How the *Stryker* both ruined and forged me. And how it still hums in the background, tugging at me after all these years.

They listened, silently weighing the intensity of their suffering against mine. They told themselves that coming to Boyd's Cove was the right choice, that only these people could truly understand what they'd endured. They cried when expected, tittered at my self-deprecating jokes, and applauded as I got off the stage. "Thanks for coming, you've been a great audience! The best, I mean it!"

But it was time. We'd shared the one thing we all had in common, and that was enough. No one at the table was looking for a new friend. Hugs from the women, handshakes from the men, and the wayfarers drifted off into what was now a blessedly half-sunny afternoon. I was about to join them when I noticed her, still sitting next to the Waylon Jennings-heavy jukebox. I'd seen her earlier, knitting quietly, just listening. The visitor hadn't spoken a word.

Like she knew I would, I walked over to her.

"Ma'am, I haven't had the pleasure yet. I'm Jenny Boyd. You are?"

She kept knitting, but glanced up. She was older, in her mid-70s. Not a brother or a spouse. A mother. A mother who had outlived her sailor son by forty years or more.

"I'm Evelyn Grace Parker."

I sized her up. A Miss Marple type. One of those Depression-era bitties, rail-thin, economical with both her charity and words.

Underestimate her at your own peril.

"Nice to meet you, Mrs. Parker. I'm about to head over to the parade now. Is there anything I can do for you?"

She set her project down—a half-finished knit cap tangled in a bundle of Sears brown yarn—and looked up. "I have a story of my own, you know."

I sat down next to her. The parade, now only minutes away, would feature the high school band, a float for the *Stryker* relatives, and two of Frank Jensen's '65 Corvettes. Another ten-minute delay was a rounding error. "Go ahead, Mrs. Parker."

"Ms. Boyd, I hail from Fort Smith, Arkansas, a little town not much different from this one. Except we don't have awful joints like this. Y'all must be raisin' skunks in the other room. My word."

I've never been to Arkansas but I'll bet there's a roadhouse or two outside of Fort Smith full of good ol' boys who'd feel right at home at The Barnacle. She might be right about the skunk-raisin' part though.

"Anyhow, back to my dead boy, Christian. We got the news in '42, just in time for Thanksgiving. I went through all the phases, just like you. In the beginning, it was the townsfolk who got my late Edgar and me through those first few years. For a while, it felt like my son's sacrifice mattered, that maybe it *meant* somethin'.

Her vowels stretched long, each word deliberate. For a moment, I thought she'd pick up her knitting, but she didn't. Her hands stayed in her lap as she continued.

"But after a few years, especially after the war, I started gettin' these nagging feelings. Premonitions, that's what Preacher Johnson calls 'em. Premonitions that somethin' wasn't quite right 'round all this *Stryker* business."

I gripped the sides of my chair as the mini-heart attack in my chest gathered strength.

"So, I start askin' the Navy for more details about that night. First few letters they shoot back pages of ten-dollar words, lots of ink sayin' nuthin'. By '50 or so, I'd tuckered 'em out. I was dead to 'em, just like Christian. No more letters. No more calls. Zippo.

"OK, so what's a mother supposed to do then? Only thing I could do. Use the brain the good Lord gave me to paint in the rest of it my own darn self. Started by askin' myself a few teasers. Like, how does a hotshot captain let an enemy ship sneak up on him in the middle of the night just a stone's throw from his home?"

She paused, giving me a moment to stew, and kept going while I stayed on radio silence.

"Here's 'nother one. Why ain't there no record of the *Stryker* in the Japanese war records? That's right, I had someone check! And tell me this: why, after all these years, am I still wakin' up in a cold sweat over my poor boy? Always the same nightmare... we're playin' checkers like we used to, and right before I wake up, he leans in and says, 'Mama, look under the table. There's somethin' under there.'"

Mrs. Parker reached out and grabbed my wrist. Her hand, speckled with anticoagulant bruises, was ice-cold.

"Ms. Boyd, I didn't haul myself all the way to this godforsaken town for nothin'. I came for one thing. One question. Is there anything—*anything at all*—you're not tellin' us? Or is Christian right? What's under there?"

Oh, dear, dear Mrs. Parker. What a simple question. And what a complicated one.

You seem like a good woman. God bless you. You've lived every mother's worst nightmare and deserve more than boilerplate condolences. You deserve a personal visit from Admiral Jim Goodman and that other squirrelly fellow to personally explain and apologize for the Navy's secrecy and deceit.

But I can't help you.

You've shoved me into a corner. Truth or lie. That's the choice. And tell me... how the hell am I supposed to decide?

We already know what Sheriff Leslie would do. She'd choose honor. *Pro aris et focis*—for altars and hearths. For Uncle Sam. For Mother Church. For dead fathers.

But me? Not so much.

If I'm going to lie for you, Mrs. Parker, you're going to have to earn it.

So I choose friendship. But not yours.

The friendship of a woman—of a hero—I've never even met.

Miyuki, I'd fib to St. Peter himself if you asked me to.

Evelyn had run out of patience with my dawdling.

"Ah, Ms. Boyd, I knew they'd ripped some pages out of this book. Indeed, child, you're sweatin' like a sinner in church. Now quit your dawdlin' and tell this old woman what she needs to know."

What she needs to know. Right. Here goes, in my own crooked brand of southern English.

"Mrs. Parker - Evelyn - from my lips to your ears, you've got the truth, the whole truth, the whole blackberry pie. I'm mighty sorry about your Christian. I'm sure he was a fine young man. And war... well, war's just fog stacked on fog. But it doesn't do anyone any good chasing conspiracies or foul play in the heat of battle."

Calling her unconvinced would be kind. Way too kind. I went back to work.

"OK, let's say there's some evil-minded intrigue at play here. We both know the government leaks like my dishwasher. It can't keep a secret this big for this long. Just look at the history: JFK's affairs, Watergate, Vietnam shenanigans."

The old lady may never have taken a deductive reasoning class at some fancy college, but her bullshit detector worked just fine. With a sarcastic "hmph," she locked eyes with me, offering another chance to make things right.

Perhaps if one truth was unavailable, a different one would suffice.

"Look, Evelyn, after all this time, here's what I can tell you. Those names on the *Stryker* monument in the town square? They're not the only casualties from that night. No, ma'am, they're just the opening credits. You and I—well, at least we're still here. But I think about all the other things that died that night, too. The weddings that never happened. The babies that were never born. The lives that never got lived.

"And the grief? That shadow that follows us, drags over every holiday, every birthday, every trip out here to Oregon? That's not just for Christian and Preston. It's for ourselves, too. For the people we were before The Cove swallowed them, before we were swallowed along with them. That person, that Evelyn? She didn't just disappear—she went straight down to the bottom, tangled with all those poor men and boys, and somehow we're left standing above, trying to breathe."

I reached for her hand.

"Hey, maybe you still recognize her. The old, pre-*Stryker* Evelyn. The light-hearted girl with the ribbon in her hair who baked biscuits and made her teachers laugh. And, once in a while, even coaxed a smile from her daddy.

"But when you think about those days, I'll bet the picture's gotten a little blurry around the edges, hasn't it? And the opposite might be true too. If that young,sassy Fort Smith Evelyn were sitting here right now, in this smelly beerhouse, would she recognize you? Or me? Not likely. And, surely, that's its own kind of catastrophe."

Mrs. Parker's eyes brimmed as I concluded.

"Thirty-four sailors died that November night. And with them went the innocence of the hundreds of us who still keep their pictures on our mantels and walk our local chapel graveyard, but have no stone to visit."

A lie followed by a truth. At least a truth according to me. Mrs. Parker nodded, not in satisfaction, but in recognition. Then she sprung one final surprise

"Ms. Boyd, you've been so kind with your time. I can't stay for your fancy parade and hotdog eating contest. But before I depart, is there anything perhaps y'all want to ask this little old lady?"

As a matter of fact...yes.

It's rare, like seeing a double rainbow after a spring shower. Or guessing right during a spelling bee. But it does happen, and it happens unexpectedly.

You meet someone. Someone who's thought it through more deeply than you. Someone who's got it figured out. Someone with real *wisdom*.

And when you do, when your pickaxe strikes that basketball-sized gold nugget, don't waste the moment. Ask your toughest questions to these Buddhas among us. You won't regret it.

"Evelyn... there is something I'd like to know. How do you live with all that pain? All that grief?"

My question didn't stump her. A laugh rattled out of her chest, dry and bitter.

"Well, dear, I'm not so sure I've really dealt with anything. I guess on the bad days I remind myself of somethin'. That the path isn't straight, it's crooked. That grievin' ain't like sprainin' your ankle. Stay off it for two weeks, crutches for two more and you're back in the garden."

I nodded as she continued.

"No, my grievin' is more like that brain disease old people get—Oldheimers. My aunt had it. It's not like she got a little worse each day, at least, not that we'd catch on. She'd lose her wits in spurts. She'd be fine all summer, and then—bam!—it's Halloween, and she thinks I'm my mother."

She paused, and made her point.

"So, grievin' ain't somethin' you can make a deal with. It don't expire like milk. Guess I figure it's not really in my control. Things happened. The *Stryker* sank. Christian's gone. And grief is gonna happen. Like you said, I'm sad 'cause I miss him. But if I'm sad, he's still here.

"So, how do I deal with sorrow? I make room for it on the couch and don't try to kick it off."

If I'm sad, he's still here. I had no words. After denying that her attendance at Preston Boyd Day did more good for me than for her, the old bird boarded the bus. No flying for her ("If it can happen to Buddy Holly and the Big Bopper..."). She'd return to Arkansas the same way she came, thank you very much. And off she went.

Maybe I chickened out on that question I asked. Should have asked a bigger one instead, the biggest one of all. Guess I'll ask you instead.

Is all this stuff just meaningless?

I could make the argument. Step one: win the ovarian lottery and be born. Step two: the world hands you six or seven decades to do whatever the hell you want: make babies, get drunk, cure smallpox. Does any of it really matter?

Too dark? Too bleak? Fine. But look it at long term. Preston Boyd Day—how ridiculous! Who gives a damn about some family drama in one of a million forgettable wars?

And what about the randomness of it all? My mother was gifted a first-class ticket on the Grief Train, with stops in Anxietytown and Schizophreniaville. So was I. I jumped off before it derailed. Margaret didn't. Why? Because I'm stronger or smarter than Margaret? Please.

But, thanks to Seaman Hayes, I've got a new thought rattling around in my brain. Maybe it was there all along. It's a little bumper-sticky, but hey, it makes sense to me.

Purpose is a lot like love. Stop looking for it, and, somehow, it finds you.

Seaman Hayes (or whatever the hell that was) blasted into my kitchen with undeniable purpose. A mission so vital, it required the laws of physics to take a coffee break just to shove the truth in my face. What was his motivation? What noble ideals could justify this chaos? Maybe justice. Maybe peace of mind. Who can say? This one's beyond even Mrs. Evelyn Parker.

What I *can* say is thai: the *Stryker*'s sacrifices *mattered* to the universe. They *meant* something. To me, the odyssey of Seaman Hayes proves our lives and our existence have purpose. Have meaning.

I know, I know, we're still a long way from home on this one. What is our purpose? Am I claiming to know the meaning of life? Have I invented some new kumbaya philosophy I can hawk on TV infomercials? Hell no!

But it's a start. One small step for man and all that. The universe has played it cool with us since we first walked upright on the savannah. *Do what you want. I don't care. I'm the infinite cosmos, indifferent to all.*

But She let her guard down, right here in Boyd's Cove. Showed a preference. Took a side. And in doing so, annihilated any lingering, bullshit excuses of mine to wait any longer.

Unlike Mick and Keith, time wasn't on my side.

Sixty Minutes

O f course it rained. Just like I'd told them it would. We're moving this show indoors after all.

But don't worry; they thought of everything.

As the director fidged a Pall Mall from the cinematographer, I gawked at The Cutter's metamorphosis: dive diner to artsy San Francisco cafe in less than an hour. CBS roadies heaved wobbly tables and mismatched chairs aside, then tore into the booths. The DIY crew was prying floor bolts loose on the west wall when Marco stormed in from the kitchen, swinging a rolling pin like a mace.

A black, floor-to-ceiling curtain dropped into place, hiding the ugly alcoves and, for the moment, America's second-oldest network was satisfied.

A soft, ambient glow suffused the interview set courtesy of a gallery of red-hot light stands and an energetic gaffer displaying all the signs of an end-stage cocaine addiction. Couldn't argue with his work though. The light frosted Harry Reasoner's salt and pepper hair perfectly as he sifted through his notes one final time, his glasses sliding down the bridge of his nose. In case you never have the pleasure, he's exactly as he appears on TV: nice, professional, and a World War II vet to boot. I was just glad they didn't send Mike Wallace.

As I joined Harry on set, I spotted the Victorian chairs the crew had lugged in that morning from the Boyd's Cove library. My threadbare blazer had been swapped for a plain evergreen

Chanel jacket, which I'd been assured "will show up on camera better." I know the term *makeup artist* is overused, but I have no better descriptor. She joked about applying my foundation a little heavy—"just in case you start to sweat during the 'gotcha' questions." She then spent most of our session dabbing my forehead while I ran through every possible way Harry could make me look foolish.

Turns out, I had nothing to worry about. He wasn't here to grill me about last year's Girl Scout cookie embezzlement scandal. Nope, this was exactly as advertised: a big-city peek into small-town America, where we look out for our neighbors and honor our past. A reminder to the Capote-and-Wintour set that enclaves like ours still exist, that we're still at their beck and call when they need a flat tire fixed on vacation or the 82nd Airborne is short a few riflemen.

He brushed me back with hardballs such as:

What makes Boyd's Cove so special?

What does it feel like to be mayor of a town named after your own father?

What's your typical day like and how do you find time for all your responsibilities?

We were winding down, and I could see the disappointment on Harry's face. He'd done his job, stayed on script, and now here we were. A few cutaways of Blanche the seagull, a handful of platitudes from me that might make the final story (though probably not), and that was it. Nothing interesting, nothing headline-worthy, no news. We'd produced the worst kind of interview: a forgettable one. As the director sent his second AC down the street for another pack of smokes, Harry posed his final question.

"Jenny, you and the entire town have put so much effort into organizing this weekend. Why do you think we hold remembrances like these? What's their value?"

I used to wonder that myself. But now I knew.

"Why do we bother with memorials like these, Harry? It's a fair question. World War II ended forty years ago. Most people today weren't alive when it happened, and even fewer have any real memories of it."

Harry perked up, liking where this seemed headed.

"I can think of three reasons why we reach back in time like this. First, we do it to honor our country—or, more precisely, the ideals it claims to uphold. Not just to honor the men who died, but the Navy, the entire military, everyone who served to protect and preserve a way of life we often take for granted."

I continued.

"The second reason is more personal: guilt. The vast majority of your audience has never heard of the *Stryker*. They'll never meet any of the surviving family members. So maybe, we tell ourselves, it's not too much trouble to light a candle once a year or carve a few names into a piece of granite to remember these poor men—men who, if fate had unwound differently, could have been any one of us.

Time to pass on Evelyn Parker's wisdom to America.

"Finally, the most important reason. And it's one that applies to all of us, because we've all experienced loss in some way. We have these remembrances as a way to keep the dead alive. To hold onto them, to keep them here with us. Because if they're in our hearts, then in some way, they're not entirely gone. They're not fully dead. Am I making sense, Harry?"

I was.

The eyes of the hardbitten correspondent sitting across from me welled up, threatening to undo all the work done in the makeup trailer. Our conversation stalled, that awkward dead air that compels your nervous aunt to fill it with chitchat. Then, he showed me, the director, and America why he'd won Emmys.

Not for what he did, but for what he *didn't* do. Resisting the human urge to step in and capture a bit of the moment for himself, he let it... hang.

He gave me air. So I breathed it.

"Harry, it seems you can relate to what I'm saying. Maybe you can also relate to another feeling I've had lately. When I look back, I sometimes ask myself: *Was this ever really my life? Or was it a life written by others? A life I simply watched go by?*

"Take the USS *Stryker*. We're celebrating today, but, in real life, everyone's moved on. The town, my best friend, even my pug Reef... meanwhile, a forty-year-old submarine still rests under the waves just west of Forget Me Knot Rock, out of sight, out of mind."

Harry smiled as I confided to the 70 million or so watching that I'd promised Reef a shout-out. I kept going, and in the process, gave Mr. Reasoner something to really smile about.

He'd have his story after all. With a twist even a chain-smoking director could love.

"Everyone's moved on. Except me. I never did. So, effective today, I'm announcing live from the Fog Cutter Café that I'm resigning as mayor. No more watching, no more wondering. I've been toying with the idea of taking a trip overseas. After all, I could use a little sunshine after all this. Don't you think, Harry?"

Texas

Dear Mrs. Alma Crocket (Hayes),

    Thanks for receiving this letter. Please allow me to introduce myself: I'm Genevieve Boyd from Boyd's Cove, Oregon. Friends call me Jenny. Hope all is well down in Texas. I've never visited but hope to someday.

    As you may know, I am the daughter of Captain Preston Boyd, the skipper of the USS Stryker that your brother Foster served on. Last month, we held ceremonies here in Boyd's Cove to honor your brother and the men he served with. I'm so sorry you weren't able to attend

    I'm writing today to apologize for not clearing something with you in advance. To mark the 40th anniversary of the Stryker sinking, the TV show 60 Minutes requested an interview with me about my memories of that terrible day and how it has shaped the town over the years. If you happened to see the segment, you may recall I specifically mentioned Foster as emblematic of the courage and bravery shown by the entire crew. One surviving shipmate described him to me as a "man of action" who "always chose the harder right over the easier wrong."

    I still live in the same house as I did as a girl, just a few nautical miles from the battle. Please don't think I'm strange, but on certain days, I can feel the presence of Foster, my father and the other men who lost their lives all those years ago.

So, thank you for listening. I wanted to reach out, at least once, to everyone who had a connection to the Stryker. In fact, next week, I'm heading all the way to Japan to tie up one last loose end.

Alma, I wish you all the best. Enjoy the enclosed photos from the ceremony.

Sincerely,

Jenny Boyd

MATRIARCH

Read on for an excerpt from Alfie & Annabelle's next story in The Fog Cutter Cafe series

Available at alfieandannabelle.com[1] and all major online bookstores.

---

1. http://alfieandannabelle.com

MATRIARCH
ALFIE & ANNABELLE

Chapter 1

I've heard all the stories.

Hard to pick a favorite. Not even sure I have one. Perhaps, as one legend goes, we were once people and our scarlet shade a solemn reminder that we all share the same blood. I never thought to ask the elders about it. Nor my mother, either.

Truthfully, I was never much interested in those sorts of questions. Let the debates rustle on in the underbrush, among the ferns and pines. We're here, and we'll always be here. That's all that matters.

And Matriarchs such as myself ensure it will always be so.

To human eyes—and even to my own—the forest seems eternal and unchanging. Yet, tribes of men have always walked among us. They scuttle below as they canvas our fallen for their shelter and canoes. Huddled along the coast and tucked deep in the valleys, they mostly keep to themselves and their gods.

But the pulse of the grove is quickening now.

This wave is fiercer than any before. Along the valley floor, the din is rising, escalating into a cacophony impossible to ignore. The woodland grows nervous, sensing a shift in its fragile equilibrium. Seeking refuge, the larger creatures retreat deep into the forest, glancing upward at me as they pass.

I remind myself my ancestors have endured catastrophes of every kind: shattered earth, rising seas, raging fires, an endless litany of disasters, their details lost to the mists of time.

So here I stand again as a new threat crests the horizon.

I just need to be strong.
And I will be.

Chapter 2

"**W**ell, we're a long way from Bryn Mawr, aren't we?" I muttered, sidestepping mud puddles as we approached the grandstand.

Why did I bother troubling myself? My lace-up Edwardian boots were already caked with coastal silt. The same boots worn to ruin these past four dreary years. New ones, you say? Then prepare for a half-day trek by Model T over a rutted cowpath down to the Woolworths in Eureka. And don't worry, I'm sure the clerk will have your size.

"C'mon, Ruthie, chin up. Look, it's stopped raining."

The townspeople tolerated me, but adored my husband. When "Sunny" Charles Wescott announced his mayoral candidacy last year, his election was as sealed as a letter already sent. I poo-pooed his "Tomorrow Starts Today" campaign slogan, but his constituents proved me spectacularly wrong. The loggers and fishermen of this backcountry Northern California town are hardy frontier folk. They demand optimism, justified or not, from their mayor—a trait that also comes in handy when soothing the grumblings of your displaced Philadelphia wife.

"Here we are, right in front."

Charles spread a wool blanket across the damp wooden bench. A sea of parasols and derby hats, the gallery bleachers were nearly full. The Arcata aristocracy of the new century was present and reporting for duty. Wives in their finest home-stitched dresses flitted about, trailed by dusty, hungry-looking husbands, a splash of high society in the wilds of Humboldt County.

In these situations, I usually rely on a stiff gin and tonic to tame my cynical propensities. But alas, not today. At previous college graduations I've attended, spirits flowed in abundant supply. But then, this was my first commencement celebrated west of the Continental Divide.

Charles was giving me that look of his: *You're the mayor's wife! Go talk to people!* Alright, alright. Time for an appearance from "sociable" Ruth.

"Good morning Margaret, and congratulations to Rebecca. She looks radiant today!"

The perennially buoyant disposition of Margaret Manion, proprietor of Humboldt Bakery, rivaled even that of my husband. Cringing, I braced for an overenthusiastic response to my insincere flattery. I was not disappointed.

"Why, thank you so much, Ruth! It's always been a dream of hers to teach. And isn't this wonderful for our little town? Having our own teacher's school here... can you imagine? And congratulations to your Dorothy as well. Top of the class, no? What will she do next?"

"Well, we'll see. She's talked about moving down to San Francisco," I lied. My heart skipped at the idea. Dorothy in an apartment on Market or Van Ness meant her mother would need to visit at least three times per year. The theater, the shopping...

Margaret interrupted my delicious daydreams.

"That *would* be exciting, wouldn't it? But my goodness, it's so far! Rebecca's teaching at a new school opening in Eureka, and Elizabeth Mead's heading down to Fortuna. I can't believe how much this area has grown since I was a child. They won't be able to call us the Lost Coast much longer!"

She laughed at her own joke as I turned away, duty fulfilled. *Keep it together, Ruth.* A couple muddy streets, a scattering of clapboard storefronts, and a four-cabin teachers' school, and suddenly we were the Upper West Side? Let's pave Arcata's Main Street first before declaring the twentieth century's arrival in Humboldt County.

Glancing at the program, I found Dorothy's name, first on the list.

Graduation Announcement

Ms. Dorothy Wescott

DAUGHTER OF CHARLES AND RUTH WESCOTT
MAGNA CUM LAUDE

FROM THE BLEACHERS, I scanned the crowd for my daughter. There she was, clustered with her fellow graduates just off-stage. My wave went either unnoticed or ignored as they chattered amongst themselves—almost certainly the latter. It was possible she might still be a *teensy* bit annoyed after I had poked her (again) at breakfast about her lack of marital prospects.

"But mother, I'm only twenty!"

"*Exactly*, my dear, exactly!"

With a sigh, I turned back to the stage. The inaugural graduation of the Humboldt State Teachers College was about to begin. The more the organizers strained to recreate the College Green at Penn, the more it resembled a county fair picnic.

Even so, I couldn't help but admire their industriousness. Monkeypod chickweed and June-blooming wildflowers ringed the outdoor stage. Electric lights draped the platform, buzzing faintly above the restless graduates. Fluffy red, white, and blue bunting cheered the scene. To top if off, the "Class of 1914" flag I'd stitched together over the past few weeks swathed the speaker's podium. A nice touch, if I say so myself.

But bunting and blossoms couldn't compete with the main attraction directly behind the stage. California's first teacher's college north of Petaluma sat tucked within a thick forest of ancient redwoods. Towering over our gathering, the giants ensured that despite the noonday sun, our ceremonies would unfold in a bone-chilling shade. When I was a little girl, I had traveled to Switzerland and marveled at the vertigo-inducing ascent of the Alps. Sheer crags thrust upward like stone skyscrapers from Zurich's flat valley floor. Here, it was a colossal fortress of wood, not ice, that sealed Arcata from the outside world.

As the school president approached the podium, I realized my prayers for a brisk ceremony were to go unanswered. In that practiced way husbands and wives secretly trash others during public events, I whispered conspiratorially into Charles's ear.

"How is it possible there are ten speakers but only fifteen graduates?"

Speaker number seven on the docket checked the program and, with mock solemnity, whispered back, "You're right, the dean must think we're in Boston or New Haven. Just sit back and relax."

As the morning dragged on, I shivered as the mountain cold ruthlessly pierced my sable coat. By the third speech, no amount of feet-stamping or husband-burrowing helped. I admired Dorothy's composure as she braved the chill from the stage. Fully exposed to the icy Pacific wind, she sat radiant, smiling as though she were sunning herself in an Adirondack chair on a July afternoon in Cape May.

"Be good, do good, and you shall have your reward!" Polite clapping whisked the dean and his platitudes offstage as he yielded to Charles. Mr. Mayor bounded up the slick grandstand steps two at a time as I steeled myself for one of his half-hour soliloquies. After thanking his "eternally patient" wife, Charles launched into one of his stump speeches I'd heard countless times. Free at last to drift, my mind wandered.

Not a good thing. Not at all. I was counting on—no, I needed—some engrossing distractions to get me through this. Ever since we arrived here, I'd sought sanctuary in mental detours. Head down, stay busy. Write those letters. Chair the First Methodist Christmas committee. And at night, a bracing nip from the brandy closet to slam the door shut.

Otherwise, they came. The real cause of my shivering. I forced myself to look up, past the stage and classrooms, into the dark, looming forest beyond.

Despite four years in Humboldt County, I'd clung stubbornly to town, never once setting foot in the surrounding wilderness. Over cigars, Charles drew incredulous laughter from his sycophants when he exaggerated that though I was a dues-paying member of the Women's Federation to Save the Redwoods, I'd never actually touched one.

Arcata chatter proposed endless theories for my "eccentricity." The leading favorite: *Philadelphia Heiress To Delicate for Dirt.* Then there was the medical hypothesis: *Socialite Allergic to Fresh Air.* Others preferred darker explanations. *She's a medium,* they whispered. *Sees trolls and goblins in the woods.*

Trolls and goblins? A much kinder terror than the one I carried..

Yet here I stood in defiance of my own edict, on the town's precipice, only stepsaway from the thing I dreaded most.

We're all experts in something. Maybe you collect stamps or can discern Roman pottery from Phoenician. My specialty is rather unique. Full disclosure: I have no credentials, no official certifications, and this accomplishment won't appear in my obituary. You'll have to take me at my word.

It's Fear. See, I know all about Fear. True Fear. Not spider phobias or nightmares of bottomless quarries filled with black, stagnant water (though you should steer clear of quarries). And certainly not those brushes with the supernatural delivered by charlatan spiritualists who trick the dead into rapping their knuckles under a table.

Please.

No, I'm self-taught in True Fear. Perhaps you are too. Maybe you've flirted in its shadows, convinced you've seen the worst It has to offer. God knows, I claim no patents or trademarks in this realm.

Here's a litmus test to know when True Fear has found you. Drumroll... What is True Fear? The absence of Hope. It arrives when you *know* what will happen next and there's not a damned thing you can do about it. Your fate is sealed. No bargaining, no clever barrister to wriggle you out on a technicality. You signed the contract. Your soul belongs to Him.

Everyday bouts of Fear fall short of this bar. The ending isn't forsworn. The tarantula startles you... but might not bite. The water is cold... but you know how to swim. Despite the peril, in these cases a flicker of faith endures. *I can fix this.* Just give me a minute to think. There's always a way.

But not always. With monstrous forests like the one engulfing me now, there's no solution. There's no bartering. I don't merely suppose their power; I know their essence. Nature doesn't take sides, they say. She's indifferent, they claim. Yeah, right.

This wilderness and I understand each other. For you, the forest may be many things: a playground, a postcard. For me, it's a murderous No Man's Land, minus the barbed wire. To leave the safety of the trenches and enter its territory invites annihilation.

Why do I know this? Ask *Her*, not me. For reasons of Her own, the entity chose to reveal herself long ago. My whole life, I've wrestled with the aftermath of our decades-old encounter. Naturally, along the way I've had my midnight moments of doubt. Fueled by Tanqueray, I've faced an unpleasant truth: history is full of crackpots magically privy to whisperings from God or the Devil that only they alone could hear. How narcissistic, how *stupid*, for me to believe *I'm* somehow special.

That *I'm* the Chosen One. I talk myself off the ledge, for a while. But my rationalization attempts always fade with the sunrise.

Call me crazy. What happened, happened.

What's the proverbial silver lining you ask? Well, I did come up with one. Yes, it's a stretch. Ready? Here it is (deep breath).

At least I know.

And I guess that's something. Clarity. Lucidity. While the rest of the world frolics in its bubble, obsessed with baseball games and stock tickers, I was granted an unwanted glimpse over the horizon. A modern-day Elijah. An unwilling recipient of an unreturnable gift.

"Here we go." I welcomed Charles's interruption. His elbow nudged my silver chatelaine purse as he motioned toward the stage. I hadn't even realized he was back. With the speaker's exhortations finally over (and quickly forgotten), the soon-to-be teachers expectantly lined up for their degrees.

Swaying, I tightly clutched his arm. "Dear, what's the trouble?" he inquired. "Do we need to leave?"

Breathe, just breathe. Reflexively, I called upon the techniques I'd used since childhood to suppress the panic. First, orient yourself. You're here, at Dorothy's graduation. Next, tighten your stomach against the oncoming waves of nausea. Here it comes... keep it down! Ignore that gagging sensation in your throat. Finally, lie to yourself that everything is fine. Just fine.

Familiar with my wifely hysterics and fragile constitution, Charles began to escort me from the stands, but I demurred. "No, no, I'm staying. I'll be fine."

Heads turned, but a reassuring nod from Charles returned everyone's attention to the stage. A box of scrolls appeared at the podium, and the Dean finally reached the part of the program we'd all been waiting for.

"Dorothy Wescott!" the master of ceremonies bellowed. I thought I'd be more emotional, but my reservoir was bone-dry. "Congratulations Ms. Wescott."

Dorothy accepted her diploma, curtsied briefly, and took the lectern for her valedictorian remarks. Happily distracted once again, I squelched my irritation at her hat choice. A straw boater for this occasion? Far too masculine. And to not even include a goose feather? But, as you might guess, my unsolicited opinion over buttered toast this morning only guaranteed the straw boater victory.

Her voice, young and clear, cut through the air and commanded our attention.

"Our pursuits of gold and status are not just materialistic trappings. They're <u>actual</u> traps. They keep us small. And so, we must all choose: a fearful life, focused on what we might lose. Or the courage to break free from our self-imposed chains in pursuit of a cause greater than ourselves."

My goodness. Apparently the Socialist party has been busy on campus.

Her closing line drew the most enthusiastic applause.

"Everyone inside for refreshments."

In unison, the grandstand crowd rose to its feet, a stampede of skirts and parasols beelining for the sponge cakes and pastry tarts. Had none of them eaten breakfast?

Head down, I made my own escape as well. But not in search of buttery croissants or hot coffee. No, my goal was shelter. Get inside, indoors, beyond the reach of the leviathans' shadows.

I can't outrun an inescapable past. Neither can you. But if I ever get the chance to put even a scrap of ground between me and this cursed wilderness, for the love of Jesus, don't stand in my way!

ACKNOWLEDGEMENTS

Annabelle and I have always loved stories and revere our storyteller heroes.

We marvel at their cleverness, their mastery of language, their ability to make our eyes widen and heart race.

So, six decades in, we planted ourselves in front of the keyboard. How hard could it be?

Of course, you already know the answer.

Climbing Mount Aspiring Author was no gentle stroll. We'd have never made it out of base camp if not for a few indispensable guides:

- Our son-in-law Bobby, a creative wunderkind and tech savant who challenged us on every detail to ensure we had a story worth telling.

- Our daughter, Lauren, the mastery gunner sergeant whose discipline kept us in cadence during the long road march.

- Austin and Tina for their suggestions and encouragement.

- Alyssa Matesic for her strategic editorial assessment.

And, above all, Annabelle, the Big Bang behind it all. Outlasting thirty years of my vague promises and increasingly-ridiculous excuses, she kept the magic real when I could not... Annabelle, all I see is you.

About the Authors

ALFIE & ANNABELLE are longtime partners in life and imagination. Drawing inspiration from their Pacific Northwest roots, they spin page-turning tales set against the haunting beauty of the Lost Coast, where mysteries lurk behind every foggy cliff and whispering forest.

Their goal? To craft stories that thrill, surprise, and maybe even make you laugh out loud. With every mystery, ghostly twist, and wild adventure, they invite readers into a world where the ordinary collides with the extraordinary.

Get lost in story with Alfie and Annabelle where everyday life meets the extraordinary, and adventure is always just a page away.

alfieandannabelle.com[1]

---

1. http://alfieandannabelle.com

www.ingramcontent.com/pod-product-compliance
Lightning Source LLC
Chambersburg PA
CBHW021359150726
47989CB00005B/2321